IN TOO DEEP

JUDE WATSON

SCHOLASTIC INC.

NEW YORK TORONTO LONDON AUCKLAND
SYDNEY MEXICO CITY NEW DELHI HONG KONG

To the High Street Irregulars
—J.W.

ISBN 978-0-545-34135-6

12 11 10 9 8 7 6 5 4 3 2 1   11 12 13 14 15 16/0

Printed in the U.S.A.   40

This edition first printing, May 2011

Book design and illustration by SJI Associates, Inc.

CHAPTER 1

The sound of rushing water filled Amy Cahill's ears. If she kept her eyes closed, she could imagine she was standing under a beautiful tropical waterfall. Unfortunately, she was hiding in an airport bathroom.

Inside a stall, she tucked up her legs and balanced her backpack on her knees. Toilets flushed, faucets ran, and suitcases on wheels trailed feet in a big hurry. The airport in Sydney, Australia, was a busy place.

Busy was good. Busy was cover. If you wanted to ditch surveillance, a bathroom could offer you a perfect opportunity. If you didn't mind crouching on a toilet for fifteen minutes.

Ditch surveillance. Only weeks ago, that would have meant not letting her little brother, Dan, read her diary. Now it was all too real. *Too* real for a fourteen-year-old.

Amy peeked over the stall. A tour group of teenagers had entered the bathroom a few moments ago, and now they chattered in French as they washed their hands and primped at the mirror. The guide cried, *"Allons-y!"* Still talking and laughing, they began to wheel their suitcases toward the exit.

It was a perfect opportunity. Amy slipped out of the stall. Smiling at a pretty French girl, she melted into the group. Women streamed in and out of the doors, and the tour group got entangled with an Australian woman with four daughters. Amy slid into the middle of the crowd as they exited.

She kept the tour group between her and the gate opposite. As soon as they headed off toward baggage claim, she ducked into a coffee bar. She scanned the corridor, searching out anyone familiar . . . or a suspicious stranger.

Everything looked normal. The only problem was that normal wasn't necessarily good. Because the *new* normal meant anyone at all could be a threat.

How about that Japanese family in super-cool footwear? The backpacking American boy and girl in matching SMELL U T-shirts? The middle-aged woman munching a muffin, the mother with a stroller, the man stopping to dial his cell phone.

Any one of them could be after her and her brother, Dan. Any one of them could be *Cahills*. Amy had never dreamed that her own last name would send such a chill down her spine.

Ever since her grandmother's will had been read, she'd been chased from one continent to another . . . by her own relatives. Her grandmother Grace Cahill had laid down a challenge to every branch of the Cahill family—either join the race for the 39 Clues and become the most powerful person in the world . . . or walk away with a million dollars. Amy and Dan had chosen the chase. Not that a million dollars wouldn't be pretty sweet. But they knew their grandmother wanted them to win.

They had no idea what they were getting into.

Sometimes Amy wondered what the scariest thing about being involved with the hunt for the Clues was. Maybe it wasn't being buried alive or almost creamed by a train or locked in a mummy's tomb. All those things had actually happened to her . . . and she'd survived. Maybe it was this—having to be suspicious of every single person on the planet. Amy and Dan had learned the hard way that any one of them could be an informer.

Would the rest of her life be like this? Looking over her shoulder all the time? *Don't wig out on me now*, Dan would say. He was three years younger, but sometimes she needed him for a reality check. Amy hurried on.

They were supposed to meet at ground transportation. As soon as their plane from Moscow had touched down, Amy, Dan, and their au pair, Nellie Gomez, split up. Instead of rushing for a taxi, they would wander the airport and give any possible pursuers the slip.

They had come to Sydney on a hunch. Back in Russia, they'd discovered that their parents had traveled under false names on Australian passports. As Amy walked down the busy corridor, she thought of the photo of her parents the Lucian Nataliya had sent them. She and Dan traded it back and forth because they both wanted to sneak looks at it. Since their parents had died in a fire at their family home, all the photographs of them had been destroyed. All except one, and Dan had lost that back in Paris.

Ever since she'd seen that photo, little pieces of memory kept drifting back to her. Suddenly, she remembered silly things, like how they'd had "breakfast for dinner" on Thursday nights, or how her mother had always carried different colored markers in her purse so they could draw on place mats if they went somewhere to eat. How one day they'd made jewels out of aluminum foil . . . and wore their crowns to the grocery store. She'd almost forgotten what a goofball her mother had been.

Her parents had been in this airport more than eight years ago. They'd walked these corridors. *Mom, Dad . . . what were you doing here?*

She and Dan could be off on a tangent. This trip might not lead to a Clue. They had no evidence that it would. But they had both known the moment they saw those passports where they were headed next. They didn't even have to exchange a word.

Their only contact in Australia was a cousin of their father's, Shepard Trent. He'd grown up with their father, so they'd always called him "uncle." They knew he lived in Sydney. There was no way their parents would have traveled here without seeing him. Uncle Shep would be their first stop.

The only problem was, they still hadn't been able to get in touch with him. His phone had been cut off. Nellie had managed to grab an address off the Internet, but they had no idea if it was current.

Amy headed for the rendezvous point. They had already decided that public transportation would be better than a taxi. If they kept a low profile, they should be able to hide in the crowds of tourists.

"Throw a roo on the barbie, mate!"

Amy winced as the bad Australian accent crashed against her ears. Then she cringed as she saw Dan dressed in an Australian bush hat and a safari jacket. He had a fake rubber snake wrapped around his neck.

"You call this is a low profile?" she hissed, swiping the hat off his head and stuffing it in the side pocket of her pack.

"What was I supposed to do in the airport shop?" Dan asked. "I had to buy *something*. Did you know that Australia has more deadly creatures than anywhere else in the world? Look at this snake—it's called a tai-pan. Its venom can kill, like, two thousand sheep. Or maybe it was two hundred. Anyway, if you get bit by one of these babies, you have to, like, get airlifted to a hospital for antivenom or else die a horrifying death right there." To demonstrate, Dan clutched the snake and began to emit choking noises, bug out his eyes, and hold his breath. *"Arrggghhhh,"* he yelled.

"Here you are, right on time. It's a miracle." Nellie walked up. She completely ignored Dan's popping eyes, red face, and strangle noises. "I like this place already, don't you? I just had the *best* lamington," she said, licking chocolate off her fingers. "Beats a donut any day."

On their last night in Moscow, Nellie had trimmed her hair with nail scissors. Now tufts of her jet-black-and-platinum-streaked hair stuck out from her head like exclamation points. She ran her fingers through it, making it stick up more than ever.

Dan fell on the floor, one leg twitching. "I bought some postcards," Nellie continued, stepping over Dan to show Amy. "Australia is gorgeous. I wonder if we have time to hit the beach."

Dan popped up. "The blue-ringed octopus!" he cried. *"Instant death!"*

"There's a bus that takes us into central Sydney," Nellie said, unfolding a map. "Then we can transfer to another to get to your cousin's place. I think that's our best bet. I mapped out the route."

"Great," Amy said.

"Even a platypus can kill you if you're not careful," Dan added. "This place is awesome."

They walked out into the bright Australian sunshine and joined the line for the bus. After the gray clouds of Russia, they were cheered by the soft breeze and blue skies.

Nellie held the cat carrier up to her face and purred at Saladin. "G'day, mate," she said in an Australian accent. "You'll be eating snapper soon, I promise."

In answer, Saladin let out a *mrrp* as the bus pulled up with a squeal of brakes. The cat-screech startled the elderly woman standing in front of them. She turned around. "What is that, dear? Some exotic Australian bird?" She peered at the cat carrier nearsightedly as she fished in her purse for a tissue.

"It's just a cat," Amy said apologetically. "He's hungry, I guess."

"Ooo, I love kitties." She pulled her red suitcase on wheels as the line of tourists shuffled forward.

Amy spoke in a low tone to Dan. "I hope Uncle Shep is still at this address. I don't know how to find him otherwise."

"We can just hang out at surf shops," Dan said. "We'll find him eventually."

Shep was a surfing bum. They'd met him when they were little, but Amy only had a hazy memory and Dan didn't remember him at all. He hadn't made it to their parents' funeral seven years before. But one of Dan's collections back in Boston was a stack of postcards Shep had sent them over the years, from places like Bali or Oahu. There was always a big wave on the front.

They boarded the bus and stowed their backpacks under their seats. The elderly woman with the red suitcase opened up her map behind them as the bus took off.

The map bounced off the back of Amy's head. "Oops, sorry dear," the woman said. "I just bopped you with the Blue Mountains."

"It's okay," Amy said. "No worries."

"Americans! I knew it! So friendly. I traveled to Kansas City once. Delicious barbecue. You're not from Kansas by any chance? No? Pity." The woman began to murmur to herself as she looked over the map. Every so often it would smack Amy on the head again, but she ignored it.

As the bus hit the city center, traffic swirled around them, and they rumbled from block to block. The change from Moscow was startling. Outside the people walked with brisk athletic strides, dressed in bright summery clothes, chatting and laughing with their companions. Everybody in Sydney seemed fit and happy.

"No wonder they call it Oz," Dan said. "This is unreal."

Nellie kept her eyes on the map and on their various stops. Amy peered at the signs.

"Doesn't Shep live near Darlinghurst?" Amy asked.

"Dude, don't call me darling," Dan said. "Ever. That's an absolute rule."

"Darlinghurst is an area of Sydney, you dork," Amy said.

"Dork, acceptable. Darling, un."

The friendly woman behind them stood up as they rolled to a stop. Dragging her suitcase and folding her map, she waved at them. "Cheerio! Enjoy your trip!"

"You, too!" Amy waved. The doors hissed shut.

Nellie consulted the map again. "We're near Circular Quay. Only a couple more stops before we transfer."

Amy leaned over to look at the map. Something was different. A familiar weight was missing. . . .

"Grace's necklace!" Amy felt weak as her hands flew up to her neck. "I lost it!"

"Are you sure?" Nellie asked, looking on the seat.

Amy couldn't answer. There was a huge lump in her throat, and she fought back tears. The necklace wasn't just a necklace. It was something that Grace had cherished. Every time Amy touched it, it brought back her grandmother's bracing presence, and she felt a connection to Grace's own courage.

The bus turned a corner as Amy frantically scrabbled on the floor. "It's not here!"

"When do you remember it last?" Nellie asked.

"When we were waiting for the bus," Amy said, thinking hard. "I tucked it underneath my T-shirt."

"It's not missing," Nellie said. "It was stolen. That old woman!"

"Really? She was so sweet. She kept hitting me in the head with the map and apologizing. . . ." Amy's mouth dropped open.

Nellie nodded. "Yup. Distracting you."

Dan began to stab at the STOP button on his armrest. "Come on. Let's go kick some little-old-lady butt!"

CHAPTER 2

Dan's backpack thudded against his spine. It felt good to run after being on a plane for a million hours. The only problem with traveling so much was . . . *traveling*.

That, and the lack of Cherry Garcia ice cream on airplanes.

Nellie passed him easily, even with Saladin's cat carrier swinging back and forth in one hand, her over-stuffed pack on her back, and their duffel slamming against her hip with every step. Nellie seemed to spend her time napping or eating, but she was in awesome shape. Nothing like having a commando for an au pair.

They reached the bus stop where the old woman had gotten off. They looked around wildly, but there was no sign of her. Pedestrians swirled around them, walking quickly, smiling, laughing, and chatting. A tall, elegant woman in green suede heels strolled over to look at an interesting building. Nobody hobbled around waving a map.

Dan spotted a splash of red in the middle of some bushes. He hurried over.

He pulled out the red suitcase the old lady had carried. It was surprisingly light. Dan flipped it open; it was empty.

Two red splotches appeared on Amy's pale cheeks, as though somebody had slapped her. Dan knew that sign. Amy was trying not to cry.

"I l-l-lost Grace's necklace. I can't believe it!" Amy collapsed on the stairs in front of a stone building.

"It could turn up," Dan said. He thought he knew how Amy felt. When he'd lost the photograph of their parents in the train tunnel in Paris, he'd cried like a little kid. Right in *public*.

Dan looked up at the building Amy had collapsed in front of. He saw the word *museum* on the sign. Normally, that would cause hives to break out on every inch of his body as he waited for his sister to drag him inside, but maybe a museum would distract her. Amy was blinking back tears so fast she was causing a breeze.

"Hey, look, a museum," he said. "Want to go in?"

"Uh, Dan? Have you noticed? It's a *museum*," Nellie said. "I think I recall you saying you'd rather have spiders suck out your eyeballs than step foot in another museum again."

Dan jerked his head toward his blubbering sister, letting Nellie know what he was up to. Nellie gave him an appreciative nod.

"That's just silly," Dan said. "Spiders can't suck out eyeballs." He thought a moment. "Though maybe they can in *Australia*. Cool. Anyway, it's the Justice and Police Museum. That could rock. Come on, Amy, let's check it out. Maybe the thief ran in here to get away from us. You can read labels," he coaxed.

Nellie sat on the stairs. "I'll wait here. They probably wouldn't let me bring in Saladin, anyway." She opened her *Dictionary of Australian Slang*. "I'll just put on my sunnies," she said, slipping on sunglasses. "I'll spit the dummy if you ankle biters take too long, but if you don't, she'll be apples!"

"Speak English, please," Dan said.

"If you take too long, dude, you're toast."

"Got it. C'mon, Amy, I bet they have weapons." Dan bounced up the stairs while Amy followed more slowly. At least she was coming.

After they paid admission, Dan paused at a wall lined with photographs of criminals from the 1890s. They all looked like they were about to eat your face for breakfast. Incredibly cool.

"Amy, listen to this! Once, this guy went missing, and then one day this shark in an aquarium coughed up his *arm*! I love this place!" But Amy had wandered off to look at a courtroom.

Dan bent over to examine the death mask of Captain Moonlight. For once, he'd found a museum that made sense.

Amy didn't get her brother. Didn't they have enough mayhem in their lives? Why did he find a place like this so fascinating?

She saw the elegant woman in the green suede shoes lean forward to examine the wall of mug shots. She looked intently at the wall, but Amy couldn't tell what she was looking at. Whatever it was, it was fascinating.

The woman turned and reached into her purse, and something about the motion pinged inside Amy. Something familiar . . . like she knew this woman. But she didn't know anyone in Australia.

By now she was used to following her instincts, no matter how strange they seemed. When the woman moved off down the hall, Amy followed. But when she turned the corner, the woman had disappeared.

A re-creation of an old cell caught her attention. Amy stepped inside. It would be so handy to have a place like this to lock away little brothers when they got obnoxious. Which would be every five minutes . . .

Suddenly, she heard the door behind her clang shut. She spun around. The woman was smiling pleasantly at her through the bars of the cell. She was beautiful, with huge amber eyes and gleaming dark hair that feathered against her face. Her skin was so smooth and perfect that it looked like a china doll's.

"Don't be alarmed. This was the only way I'd get to talk to you," she said in a British accent. Her voice was thick and creamy, as if she was holding a spoonful of yogurt in her mouth. She leaned closer, as though confiding in Amy. "We Cahills have a way of running away from each other, don't we." She winked.

Amy wanted to kick herself. The woman was a Cahill! Amy casually looked around for another exit.

"Still a worrier, I see." The woman's smile didn't waver. "You never trusted your own courage. Grace used to say that."

Amy felt a stab of pain at those words. She lifted her chin. "D-d-don't tell me about my grandmother. Who are you?"

She cocked her head and studied Amy, an affectionate smile still on her lips. "Ah, the regal stare. Now I see Grace in you. I'm Isabel Kabra."

"Ian and Natalie's mother?"

She nodded. "I've tried to stay out of the hunt for the thirty-nine clues. Tried to keep Ian and Natalie out of it, too. Unfortunately . . ." She gave an elegant shrug. "They pay more attention to their father. But things have gone too far. My children need me to step in. So, I've tracked them here."

"They're in Sydney?" That wasn't good news.

"They're checking into the Observatory Hotel right now. Natalie is probably going through the complimentary bath products, and Ian . . . well, Ian is probably thinking about you."

Amy hated the spurt of pleasure that made her heart race. Even though she didn't believe it for a minute. She rolled her eyes. "Please."

"His behavior has been disgraceful, I admit. He's afraid of his feelings. He confessed to me how much he admires you."

"Do I look like I just fell off the turnip truck?"

Isabel Kabra's eyes glinted. "What a delightful expression. Ian is all show. Underneath that superior exterior is a normal boy with his own insecurities. I have . . . complicated children." She waved a manicured hand. "I wanted to keep them away from this Cahill nonsense, believe me. We have such a lovely, fragrant life in London. Cars, clothes, a private plane. What more do they want?"

"Apparently, to be the most powerful people in the world," Amy said.

"And what does that mean, exactly?" Isabel asked. "Have you thought about that?"

She had. She still hadn't grasped it. It just seemed so unreal, like something out of a movie or a video game.

"What would be the source of your power?" Isabel asked softly. "And how would you wield it? I mean, really," she said, chuckling, "a fourteen-year-old and an eleven-year-old ruling the world? You have to admit it's rather ridiculous."

"Wow," Amy said. "Can you do that again? I mean, insult me in a really nice way?" Amy couldn't believe the cool, sardonic voice was her own.

"I don't mean to be insulting," Isabel said in a kind tone. "Just realistic. Do you think that even if you win the hunt for the clues, the danger you face would be over?" She shook her head. "It would be just the beginning. One only has to look at history to see that. My children are poor students. But you are a great researcher. You know that history has proved that every conqueror has a fall."

Why does she know so much about me? Amy wondered. *I know nothing about her.*

"I was so fond of your parents," Isabel said. "They had such beauty and promise. . . . I was devastated when I heard about the fire. Maybe if they had lived, things would be different today. Maybe the Cahills would be a little more . . . civilized. But as it is, we have only one hope. The Lucians."

Amy snorted. "There's a shocker. You're a Lucian."

"Naturally, I feel the Lucians are best equipped to handle ultimate power. We combine the best qualities of all the Cahills. We are leaders. We have a global network in place. But you and your brother . . . you're so alone. Your parents are gone, Grace is gone, there's no one to protect you. I only want the little girl I remember — the girl in the nightie I cuddled in my lap so long ago — to grow up safe. If you only knew what . . ." She hesitated.

"What?"

Footsteps echoed down the hallway. Isabel turned in the direction of the noise.

"Trust me," she whispered. And then she hurried away.

CHAPTER 3

Amy pounded on the cell door. "Hello? Help?" she yelled.

Dan appeared and looked inside the bars. "Whatever you did, I'll always stand by you," he said.

"Don't be a dweeb. Get the guard and open this door!" Amy yelled.

Dan pushed on the door, and it slowly swung open.

Amy blinked. Why had she thought the door was locked? Come to think of it, Isabel had never said that it was.

She felt her legs trembling. She was more shaken up than she wanted to admit.

"C'mon," Dan said. "I found this awesome collection of knives. One of them still has bloodstains on it!"

"Dan, Isabel Kabra was here," Amy said.

"*Isabel* Kabra? Multiplying Cobras. Which one is that?"

"Ian and Natalie's mother!"

"Oh, man. Those kids have a *mother*?"

"She was almost . . . nice," Amy said. "She actually *apologized* for Ian."

"Too late. Her kids are the hounds of suck."

"She said the Lucians should win—"

"Duh."

"—and that I should trust her. She was about to tell me something."

Dan made a face. "Let me guess. Go home, little children, this game is too dangerous for you, you're going to lose. Blahbaddy blah. We've heard it a million times since we started. So which branch got the *originality* gene? They all sound the same."

Amy decided to leave out the part about Ian really liking her. She wasn't buying it, of course. But Dan *definitely* wouldn't buy it.

"She said she met me when I was little, but I don't remember her at all," Amy said.

Dan was barely listening. "We'd better get outside or Nellie is going to have a freak attack."

As they walked toward the exit, Amy stopped in front of the wall of mug shots. "Why was she here?" she wondered. "It wasn't just a coincidence. She stopped here, at the mug shots. She was leaning in, right—" Amy stopped. "Dan! One of the mug shots is missing!"

Neatly cut out from behind the Plexiglas, one small photograph was gone.

"Now we'll never know who it was," Amy said.

Dan closed his eyes. Amy knew he was going over the photographs in his mind. Even though there were about a hundred on the wall, she knew he'd remember the one that was missing.

"Follow me," he said. Amy hurried after him to the gift shop. There was a framed poster on the wall showing the same criminal faces. Dan put his finger on one, a youngish man with dirty hair and a blank expression. One side of his face showed white scars from his forehead to his chin. "Him."

"Bob Troppo," the clerk behind the register said.

"Is that some sort of Aussie greeting?" Dan murmured to Amy. He waved. "Bob Troppo!" he called.

The clerk came from around the counter. "The bloke you're looking at. He was called Bob Troppo. Nobody knew his real name because he never spoke. 'Gone troppo' is an Australian expression for someone who's lived in the tropics so long he's gone a bit weird. He lived in Sydney in the 1890s."

"What did he do?" Dan asked. "Feed someone to a croc? Tie him to the railroad tracks?"

"He tried to assassinate Mark Twain."

Amy and Dan exchanged a glance. Mark Twain was a Cahill descendant. He was a Janus, the clever, artistic branch.

The clerk, a burly young man in khaki shorts, leaned against the counter. "Twain was on a lecture tour, you see, back in 1896. Troppo was seen talking to him in an alley outside the hall where he spoke. Apparently, they had words, and Troppo smashed him on the shoulder with a cane!"

"That doesn't sound like an attempted assassination," Amy said.

"The cane had a knife concealed in it. That was enough to convict him, especially since he never spoke a word in his defense. Anyway, he escaped in a totally ingenious way." The clerk leaned forward as if he was about to impart a secret. "He was in jail, but he had the job of cleaning the floors at night, you see. So every night he scraped the wax off the wood and kept it in his cell. Then he made a wax impression of a key! Is that clever or what?"

Dan and Amy exchanged another glance. They knew each other so well and had depended on each other for everything for so long that they could communicate without speaking. *Ekaterina?* The Ekat branch was ingenious and inventive.

"What happened to him?" Amy asked.

"Nobody knows. Rumor has it that he took off into the bush. Would you like to buy some handcuffs? A book?"

"Handcuffs?" Dan asked.

Amy pulled on his shirt. "No, thank you. We have to be going. Thanks for the story!"

Amy and Dan walked out of the shop and headed for the door.

"Bob Troppo sounds crazy," Amy said.

Dan nodded. "Gotta be a Cahill."

"But what does Isabel want with him?" Amy wondered. "Is he the reason the Kabras are in Sydney? Or . . ."

". . . is it us?" Dan asked.

Amy, Dan, and Nellie stood in front of a metal door. There was no nameplate, just a grimy button that could be a doorbell. The building was made of corrugated steel and brick, with long shuttered windows. It looked like a warehouse.

"Maybe this isn't it," Amy said, suddenly nervous.

"It's the address," Nellie said. She pressed the bell.

They waited. Amy shifted from one foot to the other. She felt heat rise in her cheeks. How crazy was it to travel halfway around the world and show up at someone's door? Someone who hardly managed to stay in touch with his own cousin and best friend?

"Can you say 'wild goose chase'?" Dan whispered after a few moments.

"We should go," Amy said. She took a step back.

"Yo!" The voice came from inside.

A moment later, the door was flung open. A middle-aged blond man stood looking inquisitively at them. Everything about him seemed sun bleached, from his hair to his yellowish T-shirt to the golden hair on his tanned, muscular forearms. He was wearing board shorts, and his feet were bare.

"G'day," he said pleasantly. He used the Australian greeting they'd heard several times today, but he still had his American accent. "Can I help you?"

"Uncle Shep?" Dan asked. "It's Dan and Amy. This is our au pair, Nellie Gomez."

Shep looked puzzled.

"Dan and Amy *Cahill*," Amy added. "Y-your cousins." How awkward was this? He didn't even recognize them!

Shep looked stunned for a moment. Then a grin lit up his face. His light blue eyes almost disappeared, and lines radiated out from the corners.

Amy felt as though she'd been punched in the stomach. She had blurred memories of her parents, but seeing that grin, suddenly her father came back to her. He used to smile that way just before he scooped her up in one of his big hugs. She felt tears sting her eyes, and she quickly looked away, as though she was checking the address.

"You've got to be kidding me. Dan and Amy?"

"We were in the neighborhood," Dan said.

Shep stepped forward so quickly it alarmed them. But he embraced Dan, almost crushing the breath out of him. Then he hugged Amy.

"Well, stone the crows! Come in, come in!" He ushered them inside.

The house was just one huge open room divided by sofas and stacks of shelves. The long far wall was filled top to bottom with shelves crammed with books. Amy longed to explore the titles. Another wall was all glass and led to a patio. Groupings of furniture separated the room into living, dining, and playing areas, apparent by the piles of audio equipment, the guitars, keyboards, surfboards, computers, pinball machines, three carousel horses, and a Foosball table. Brightly painted wooden crates held items that spilled out onto the floor—clothing, more books, athletic equipment, DVDs, and computer parts.

"Wow," Dan said. "This place could have been designed by me."

"Have a seat." Shep quickly rushed to push a load of surfing magazines, T-shirts, and sandals off a couch. "What are you doing in Sydney? Last I heard you were living with your aunt."

"Um, we still are," Amy said. "Technically. But we're on vacation. Sort of."

"I see. I think. Man, you two sure have grown."

"Well, it's been eight years since you saw us."

He nodded, and the brightness left his gaze. "I know."

Amy, Dan, and Nellie sat on the couch.

Shep took a seat on the coffee table made out of a surfboard in front of them. "Listen, first off, I'm sorry about not keeping in touch," he said. "I'm just not the keep-in-touch sort."

"It's okay," Amy said. But suddenly, she realized that it really wasn't. They didn't know Shep, but he was their father's closest relative and best friend. Except for postcards and a couple of Christmas cards of kangaroos in Santa hats, they'd barely heard from him.

"It's not okay." Shep looked down at his clasped hands. "I was sorry to hear about Arthur and Hope. Devastated, actually. I didn't get the message until after the funeral that they . . . were gone. I called, but some old bat kept telling me you had enough to worry about. That wouldn't be your auntie, would it?"

"That would be her," Dan said grimly.

"She never told us you called," Amy said.

"Do you have a place to stay? I've got plenty of room. No beds, but plenty of room." He grinned at them, and Amy had a weird sensation like she wanted to cry and laugh at the same time. He looked so much like her father.

"We tried to call," Amy said.

"I just have a mobile now. Sorry I'm such a hard bloke to find."

Amy leaned forward. "We wanted to ask you about our parents' last trip here. Did you see them?"

"See them? Of course I did. That would be about . . . five years ago?"

"Eight, actually."

"Yeah, time flies." Shep shook his head. "It was the last time I saw Artie."

Artie? Nobody ever called their father Artie.

Saladin *mrrped* loudly. Shep leaned over. "Hello there, Mister Chow," he said. "You look hungry. Would you like to get out of there?"

"Careful, he's been in there awhile," Nellie said. "And he's not so good with strange—"

Shep was already lifting Saladin out and twining him around his shoulders like a fur stole. Saladin blinked, then purred happily. "Bet you'd like a dish of something," Shep said to the cat. He crossed to the kitchen area. He poured water into a shallow bowl and stuck his head in the fridge. "How about some barramundi?"

"Barracuda?" Dan asked.

"Barramundi," Nellie said. "It's a delicious fish."

"He only likes snapper," Amy said.

"Then he'll love barramundi," Shep said. "Best fish in the world." He forked some into a bowl and put it on the floor. Saladin smelled it, looked up at Shep, and gave a great, happy me-WOW!

They all laughed as Saladin dived in.

"I practically grew up with your dad," Shep said, crossing back to them. "Our mothers were cousins and best friends. They grew up together, and Artie and I did, too. Until we were twelve. Then my mom and dad got divorced and the next thing I knew I was in Oahu with my mom. Art and I tried to stay in touch, but . . . well, twelve-year-old boys don't make the best pen pals. But every time I saw him, we just picked up where we left off."

"Do you know where our parents went when they were here?" Dan asked.

"Sure. I ferried them around."

"You have a ferry?" Dan asked hopefully.

"Better than that," Shep said with a laugh. "A plane. A sweet Cessna Caravan, so—" His cell phone trilled, and he reached into the pocket of his shorts. He listened intently for a moment, said "Right-o," and hung up.

He jumped to his feet. "We've got to get out of here. Now!"

CHAPTER 4

Amy, Dan, and Nellie were used to quick exits. Dan stuffed his feet back in his sneakers. Amy leaped over the back of the couch. Nellie charged for the door, opened it, and waited until Amy and Dan were clear.

Shep leaped into the Jeep parked outside. "Get in!" he roared.

A surfboard stuck out of the back, and Dan and Amy had to wedge themselves in next to it while Nellie swung into the front seat. Shep took off with a squeal of tires.

Nellie leaned closer to Shep as they rocketed over the bumpy road. "What happened? Where are we going?"

"Bondi, of course!" Shep yelled over the rushing wind. "Surf's up!"

"Surf's up?" Nellie asked incredulously. "I thought the place was going to blow!"

Dan crashed back against the seat in relief. Amy blew out a breath.

"You've got to drop everything when the call comes," Shep said. "I have to say, you three are aces at clearing out."

"We used to be fire drill monitors at school," Dan said lamely.

"Don't worry, there're plenty of shops," Shep yelled over the rushing wind. "You can pick up your gear there. And I've got plenty of surfie mates with long boards, short boards, body boards — we'll set you up."

"I never understood surfing," Nellie said. "I'm a New England girl. Why jump on a board and get creamed by giant waves? I'd rather just swim."

Shep chortled. "You'll love it. Just watch out for the bluebottles, and you'll be fine."

"Can they kill you?" Dan asked hopefully.

"Nah, but the pain is excruciating."

"Cool!"

Within a few minutes, Shep pulled into a space in front of a small surf shop. Soon he was cheerfully directing them to the proper gear and slapping down a credit card. Now dressed in board shorts and tops, they followed him down to a wide beach with rolling high surf.

"The waves look awfully big," Amy said.

Dan was glad that somebody besides him had said it.

"Don't worry. Excellent lifeguards. Don't wave if you get into trouble, just raise your arm. Hey, there are my surfies!"

Shep waved at a group that was passing around bottles of juice and sandwiches. They all looked tanned and athletic, both men and women, with sun-bleached hair like Shep's. Surfboards were resting on the sand or stuck in it like standing stones.

"There he is!" one of the men called. "Took your time getting here, mate."

"What have you got there, some shark biscuits?" another one called.

"Did they just call us *shark* food?" Amy asked, gulping.

"Don't pay them any mind. *Shark biscuit* just means a beginner." Shep strode forward. "These are my rellies Amy and Dan, and their au pair, Nellie. They're going to learn how to surf like an Aussie."

"Choice," one of the girls said. "I've got a boogie board you can borrow."

Shep grinned and tucked his board under his arm. "Come on, you three. I'll give you a quick lesson. And don't worry about the sharks—just stay between the flags."

"Sharks," Nellie muttered. "Better on a plate. Sauce on the side."

They spent twenty minutes trying to get the hang of the boogie boards. Nellie caught on almost immediately, but Amy kept falling off and getting dunked in the surf. She'd wind up yards down the beach and come up sputtering, having swallowed half of the Pacific Ocean. Dan kept laughing at her and getting smacked in the face with a wave. It was the most fun he'd had since he'd Fed-Exed his dead spider collection to his piano teacher.

"I think you've got the hang of it now," Shep told them after awhile. "If you don't mind, I'll paddle out with the long board for a bit."

"I'm going to sunbathe," Nellie said.

Nellie headed in, and Shep paddled out. Dan and Amy positioned themselves for the next wave. Amy pushed her hair out of her eyes and grinned. That worried look that made her eyebrows come together was gone. Dan caught a wave at the perfect point. He yodeled with happiness.

When he finally came into shore, he sprang up laughing. But his grin faded when he saw a family in matching bright yellow board shorts and blue goggles start to splash into the water with long surfboards.

Holts. Muscle-bound dimwits on parade.

Dan towed his board as he timed a swim out past the breakers to where Amy still lay on her board, rocking with the swells.

"We have company."

Amy scanned the beach. "Oh, no. Quick, let's—"

But it was too late. Eisenhower Holt had spotted them. He pointed a thick finger in their direction. "Game on!" he bellowed over the crashing surf.

"What do you think they want?" Dan asked. "Besides to drown us?"

"Hamilton wouldn't," Amy said uncertainly.

They had struck up a temporary alliance with Hamilton Holt in Russia. They'd even shared a Clue with him. But that didn't mean they were friends.

"The Hammer is scared of his daddy," Dan said. "*I'm* scared of his daddy. You can't show fear to a Holt, though. They smell fear, and it tastes like chicken." He smacked the surface of the water. "Bring it on!" he yelled back at Eisenhower.

Eisenhower flopped onto his board awkwardly, but as he began to paddle through the surf, he moved powerfully fast. "You owe us!" he yelled. "You sent us to *Siberia*! That wasn't *fun*! Now we need some answers."

"We gave you a clue!" Amy shouted.

"Big deal! We would have found it anyway!"

"Dream on!" Dan yelled. "You couldn't find a clue if it bit you on the nose and hung on until Thursday!"

Eisenhower beckoned to his family. "Hit the waves, crew!" Reagan and her twin sister, Madison, jumped on their boards and began to paddle. Mary-Todd followed more slowly, eyeing the breaking surf. Hamilton brought up the rear.

"What should we do?" Amy bit her lip.

"Catch the next wave," Dan said. "C'mon!"

They flipped over on their boogie boards and looked behind. A set of waves was approaching, and they paddled hard. But they couldn't get up enough momentum. The first wave picked them up, but they ended up sliding over the lip instead of being carried toward the beach.

Eisenhower Holt emerged through the breaking wave, his powerful arms propelling him toward them. Within seconds, he had smashed his board into Dan's. Dan felt himself flying off and hitting the water. When he came up for air, Eisenhower's big hand was on his head. Dan felt himself going under again.

He came up sputtering.

"Stop it!" Amy shouted. She threw herself off her board and began pounding on Eisenhower's leg. "He has asthma!"

Amy might have been a delicate frond of seaweed brushing his leg for all the attention he gave her pounding fists. Eisenhower ducked Dan again. Dan felt his lungs squeezing. When he came up, he hung on to Eisenhower's board and panted. His own board floated nearby.

Eisenhower held his meaty palm over Dan's head. "Give me a hint or he goes under."

They had drifted down the beach and were closer to the big sets rolling in. A wave was forming.

"Dive," Dan said to Amy.

"Dive?" Eisenhower asked. "What kind of a hint is—"

Dan and Amy dived. The last thing they heard was Mary-Todd screaming, "Honey, watch—"

Dan felt the powerful pull of the wave, but he was deep enough to escape it. He came up, taking a breath. Amy emerged next to him, treading water.

Eisenhower hadn't had time to maneuver himself

or dive. The wave smacked into him and took him, his surfboard flying in the air. They only saw flashes of bright yellow as he tumbled. A lifeguard stood up with binoculars, watching.

Eisenhower ended up on the beach, his face in the sand. Mary-Todd had caught the wave in, and she hurried toward him. Eisenhower got up, red with anger. He shook off Mary-Todd's arm, struggled back to his board, and charged back into the surf. All the Holts began to power-paddle their way out to the breakers again. They moved like sharks, slicing through the water with grace and speed.

Shep paddled up to Amy and Dan, towing their boogie boards. "He got caught in the rinse cycle, all right. Deserved it, too. Does he think it's funny to dunk a kid? Friend of yours?"

"A really obnoxious family we met on the plane," Amy said. "Think you and your friends can out-maneuver them?"

"Seriously?" Shep said.

The rest of his surfing buddies came near as Shep gave a whistle. They paddled over in quick strokes.

"My rellies have a slight problem with those yellow tourists over there," Shep said. "They're trying to horn in on our territory, for one. And they're a bit nasty, to boot."

Shep's friends all grinned. "Let's go," one of them said.

"I'll catch you later," Shep told his friends. He turned to Amy and Dan. "Just paddle along behind me. I'll get you clear."

They paddled behind Shep but couldn't resist twisting to watch his friends. Three of them caught the next wave and headed straight for the Holts, who were paddling out to the break. With expert control of their boards, Shep's friends plowed right through the group. Eisenhower fell off his board and came up sputtering. Amy saw Hamilton start to laugh, then quickly dive into a wave instead.

The surfers easily cut back over the wave and paddled out again. A red-faced Eisenhower swam after his board, shouting at his children and his wife.

The Holts spread out as another wave rolled in. Two of Shep's friends paddled quickly. Amy lost sight of them as the wave curled, but in another moment she saw them riding the wave . . . straight toward Eisenhower. Eisenhower's eyes bugged out as he saw two surfers skimming down the wave at him. He tried to maneuver his board away, but it flipped over and flew into the air. They lost sight of Eisenhower until the shallow water, where he came up gasping. His board smacked him on the head.

Dan and Amy burst out laughing.

"All right, we're going to catch this wave," Shep said.

Amy gulped. The swell looked enormous. "That one?" she squeaked.

"Just paddle as fast as you can. Then ride this baby in. NOW!"

Amy dug her fingers into the sea, paddling as fast as she could. She felt the wave suck her backward. And then suddenly, she felt the lift as the wave caught her board and propelled her forward. Shep leaped to his feet and glided down the wave, shaking the water out of his hair.

Amy decided she wasn't going to die. She heard Dan yell "Ya-hoo!" as the wave brought them in. She rolled off the board, her whole body tingling.

Amy scanned the ocean behind her. Reagan and Madison were paddling out. Mary-Todd was hanging on to the edge of her board. Hamilton was beyond the swells, rocking gently on the waves. When Eisenhower saw that Amy and Dan had hit the beach, he tried to turn around, but Shep's friends ringed him on their long boards. He got hit in the face with another wave.

Shep's friends waved good-bye as they headed up the beach. Nellie was already standing, waiting for them. Laughing, they ran to Shep's Jeep. He tossed towels at them, still chuckling.

"Nothing like a band of surfies to teach some manners," Shep said, satisfied.

CHAPTER 5

Irina Spasky sat on the steps of the Sydney Opera House. The roofline of the famous building surged forward, mimicking the dancing waves of the harbor. The sun was a golden disc in a sky as blue as a Fabergé egg. Tourists and locals walked by, contented people enjoying a lovely day in a beautiful city.

You are all doomed, she thought.

If she were to stop these people and ask *Where are you from?* — although of course she would never be so friendly — the answers would be easy. Sydney, Tokyo, Manila, Los Angeles. Tourists from so many cities and small towns in so many countries. Sometimes their countries got along, and sometimes their countries did not, and that was why there were governments and diplomats and, occasionally, wars. That's the way the world worked. They thought.

But where did the real power lie? In the shadows. In the shadows, there were no borders. Everything dissolved into gray.

For a Cahill, countries and boundaries were

meaningless. Only branches mattered. One branch could rule the world.

Blin! Irina had come to grudgingly admit that Grace had done it after all. She had contrived a way to find the 39 Clues. A hunt that had been going on for hundreds of years, but at last it would be over. Irina had little doubt of it now. She felt it in her Russian bones.

Then what?

Irina had always believed with every cell in her body that the Lucians were best equipped to win. She had believed in Vikram Kabra once. But the years had corrupted that bright young man she'd known at Oxford. He had met the beautiful Isabel and married her. Once upon a time, if those two walked into a room, it seemed to shine and spin with their particular dazzle. Irina remembered days and nights of falling under their spell — Vikram's warm voice, his keen intelligence, Isabel's shrewdness and humor.

Once upon a time . . . yes, every fairy tale began that way.

When she'd met them, she'd already been a KGB agent for two years. She'd joined the KGB at sixteen — their youngest operative — and had been trained and educated to become an exchange student at Oxford. She had met Vikram, and they'd become friends almost immediately.

Irina hadn't known it, but she was a Cahill. She had been recruited by the KGB *because* she was a Cahill. Her superior had also been a Lucian, and she had been sent to Oxford, where Vikram had been waiting.

It had been Vikram who had shown her the Cahill world, told her about the Lucians. She had continued in the KGB, but as the years went on, she did more and more jobs for Isabel and Vikram as they ascended the ranks of the Lucian elite.

She had believed in them. She had believed in their ruthlessness. She'd believed in her own. It was *necessary.* The Lucians must win at any cost.

And then just a few days ago, she'd almost killed two people who got in her way.

Amy and Dan Cahill. *Children.*

What had become of her?

Irina put a finger on her twitching eye, but it would not stop jumping.

Irina stared at the bright, pretty world. She was not used to having doubts. They made a person feel so . . . *unmoored.*

Right now she had a job. Amy and Dan were in Sydney. Isabel herself had gone with the Lucian team to tail them from the airport. It had been years since Isabel had acted as an agent, and it was typical of her to jump in and risk the careful planning. Her ego came into play, as it always did. She wanted to prove that she was still an expert at disguise. So she'd pretended to be an elderly woman, and then, just for fun, she'd stolen Amy's jade necklace. Which meant she had to leave the bus, which meant that now Irina had a problem. She had no idea where Dan and Amy were staying, and

IN TOO DEEP

37

Isabel snapping *Find them!* in her face wasn't helping.

What was Isabel up to? The fact that she'd actually left her mansion in London to fly all the way here was troubling. Isabel and Vikram liked to control things from afar. Isabel claimed that jet lag gave her wrinkles.

Not that you have to worry about such things, she'd told Irina with a laugh. *Obviously, you don't care about your appearance.*

This was true, but it was still insulting. Once, Irina had been attractive. Some had called her beautiful. One person in particular.

Irina's eye twitched. That was long ago.

So much had gone wrong in Russia. Amy and Dan, she was sure, had found the Clue. She'd been certain that they were being helped, but still. . . . What they were able to accomplish on their own . . . Dan on that motorcycle! Amy driving a car! Irina quirked her lips, but she didn't allow the smile to escape.

She rose to her feet. *Enough.* She had a duty to do. If only the memories would stop! A little boy walked by between his parents, clutching a stuffed animal, something gray . . . a monkey? No, a puppy. It was only a puppy.

Irina felt the nerve in her eye shiver, and she reached up a hand to still it. A group of young people thought she was waving to them, and they waved back.

Scowling, she jammed her black sunglasses on. How she hated Australia! It was such a *cheerful* country.

CHAPTER 6

It was hard to imagine, but it was still afternoon. Jet lag was beginning to set in. But there was so much still to talk about. Shep made tea, and they sat around a table on the patio off the kitchen area. The exhilaration of out-surfing the Holts had drained away. Now they wanted answers.

Saladin jumped up on Shep's lap. Shep stroked him absentmindedly as he talked.

"I did get the idea that Art and Hope's visit was more than a pleasure trip," he said. "I guess Art was doing some sort of mapping connected to his mathematical genius thing. He was always interested in geography as a kid. Always poring over maps. It's strange how I was the one who traveled the world. I think he liked going places in his head." Shep smiled. "Not your mother, though. She was ready for anything."

"So where did they go?" Amy asked.

"Normally, I'd space that kind of thing out," Shep admitted. "I fly a lot of people a lot of places, you see. That's what I do for a living—I fly tourists around the outback. But that trip, I remember. Let's see . . . I flew them to Adelaide, dropped them off for a few days while I went on to Perth. Then I flew back, picked them up, and we all went up to the Top End. Darwin. Hey, I bet I still have their itinerary. Lucky for you, I'm the original pack rat. I don't throw anything away."

Gently, Shep dropped Saladin on Dan's lap and got up. Through the open door, they could see him rummaging in one of the colorful bins. "Well, would you look at this," he muttered, tossing away a tennis racket. "That's where that went. Never could stand tennis. Now, I know it's in here someplace. . . . Aha!"

Shep came back, a battered leather jacket over one arm and a thick book in the other. He handed the jacket to Amy. "Here's something of your mother's. She picked it up at a vintage shop in Darwin. At the last minute she left it with me. She said she had enough baggage to carry. Sure she would want you to have it."

It was warm on the patio, but Amy let the weight of the jacket remain on her lap. Her fingers ran over the leather. Her mother had picked this out. Slipped her arms in the sleeves. Amy would hug it if she could, but she was too embarrassed.

Shep held up the book. "This is my logbook from that year. Let's see now . . ." He leafed through it. "I thought so. They gave me an itinerary, just in case, they said. Here." He held out a piece of paper. Amy recognized her mother's neat handwriting in the purple ink she liked to use.

Miami	Calcutta
Natal	Rangoon
Dakar	Bangkok
Khartoum	Singapore
Karachi	Darwin

"They went to all these places?" Amy asked.

"Round-the-world trip, I guess," Shep said.

Dan peered over her shoulder. "How come Sydney isn't there? And Adelaide?"

"I guess I was the pleasure part of the trip," Shep said with a grin.

Amy put her finger on Miami. "I remember now!" she exclaimed. "They brought us along on the first part of the trip. We stayed in a hotel on the beach. Dan, you were only about three. Grace came with us, too. I remember crying so hard when they left. I thought I'd never see them again. . . ."

Amy's voice trailed off. She remembered her six-year-old self crying as though her heart would break, feeling abandoned. She'd been holding Grace's hand, and it scared her when she saw that Grace was crying, too. Grace never cried. They had stood in the lobby of the hotel, watching through the glass doors as her parents climbed into a taxi. She remembered that glass wall between them, so that no matter how hard she cried her mother couldn't hear her.

"I don't remember a thing," Dan said.

"No, you were too young," Amy said. "They were

gone for a long time—I mean, it seemed long, but it was probably about a month. Grace stayed with us." Amy had a sudden memory of Grace sitting at the window, looking out at the yard. Her grandmother had looked so worried. To Amy, it seemed that Grace had felt exactly as she did, lonely and scared. She had climbed into Grace's lap. *They'll be home soon,* Grace had murmured against her cheek.

Had Grace been trying to reassure herself . . . as well as Amy? Had Grace been just as afraid as her granddaughter?

They had to have been on a Cahill mission. It was no pleasure trip. They wouldn't have left Dan and Amy for that long if they didn't have to. Amy knew that as a solid truth in her heart.

"Surprised me when Arthur became a professor," Shep said. "I would have thought anything but that."

"What do you mean?" Dan asked. "What did you think he'd become?"

"Lion tamer," Shep said, putting his empty mug down with a smack. He grinned. "Acrobat. Professional race car driver. Bush pilot, like me."

Dan hooted with laughter. "You've got to be kidding me."

"When we were kids, Artie was the daredevil," Shep said. "He was always egging me on. Built an obstacle course for our bikes. Built a tower out of boxes so we could jump into the lake. Once we built a slide from the garage roof. Artie always went first."

"Dad?" Dan's voice was close to a squeak. "Awesome!"

Amy looked at Dan. He was sitting up straight in his chair, his eyes sparkling. Hearing about their father always made him happy. Why did it make her so sad?

When you lose your parents, the sadness doesn't go away. It just changes. It hits you sideways sometimes instead of head-on. Like now. Amy hadn't expected to suddenly feel like bursting into tears just hearing that her dad had been a daredevil when he was younger . . . just like Dan.

"Your dad, though—he was smarter than me. He did his schoolwork. He was always interested in puzzles, too, in figuring things out. I moved to Hawaii and discovered waves, and I was a lost cause." Shep grinned cheerfully at them. "I've been traveling around the world ever since. Until I landed here in Oz."

"Awesome," Dan said again. Amy could see that he'd found a new hero.

"Now it's your turn." Suddenly, Shep's blue gaze was penetrating. "What are you doing in Australia?"

Amy spoke quickly, before Dan could say anything. It wasn't as though they couldn't trust Shep, but it would be better for him if he didn't know anything about the chase for the 39 Clues.

"We're on vacation," she said. "And we're tracing our family history for a school project. Have you ever heard of Bob Troppo?"

"Can't say I know him. Does he live in Sydney?"

"No, he was a famous criminal from long ago, like the 1890s," Dan said. "He has these really fierce scars on his face. He was in jail in Sydney and he escaped to the outback."

"Where?" Shep asked. "The outback is a pretty big place, you know. Thousands and thousands of miles." He raised his eyebrows. "The land of the Never Never."

Amy and Dan looked at each helplessly. They didn't know.

"Doesn't seem like you have much to go on," Shep said genially. "That's just the way I like it. You find out more that way."

"But where do we start?" Amy wondered.

"Well, I have a mate who does outback tours from out of the Red Centre," Shep said. "Uluru, Coober Pedy, the Alice."

Dan and Amy had no idea what he was talking about. He fished in his pocket for his cell phone. "I can give him a call and ask if he knows anything about your Bob Troppo." He dialed a number and waited, then shrugged and hung up. "No answer. Jeff's not keen on voice mail. But he'll turn up eventually."

They didn't have time for eventually.

"So," Dan said. "You have a plane."

"That's really cool," Amy said.

Shep laughed. "Hold on, I'm starting to get this," he said. "You want me to fly you to the outback?

Meet up with my mate and see what you can find?"

"It's not like we'd want you to feel obligated or anything," Amy said, feeling defensive.

"It really wasn't that bad, being brought up by an evil aunt," Dan said. "Except for that whole part about being chained up in the basement."

Shep rolled his eyes, but then the humor drained from his face. "I wasn't much of an uncle to you two, was I."

"No worries," Dan said. Amy could see that in Dan's eyes, Shep could do no wrong.

Shep cleared his throat. He stood up and stacked the mugs on a tray. "Well," he said, "at least I can fly."

Dan hooted with laughter. "You mean you'll do it? You'll fly us, like, a thousand miles, just because we asked?"

"A couple of thousand. Welcome to Australia, mate," Shep said with a grin.

He disappeared inside, whistling.

Dan leaned over to Amy. "We could have gotten him as a guardian. Instead, we got Aunt Beatrice the Bloody. Life stinks."

Nellie laughed. "Those are the breaks, kiddo. Anyway, now you've got me — Nellie the Magnificent." Nellie's phone rang, and she was smiling as she answered it. Her face changed as she listened. She put her hand over it. "It's Ian Kabra," she said to Amy. "He wants to talk to you."

CHAPTER 7

Amy felt their eyes on her as she took the phone. Her face grew hot and she turned so that Dan couldn't see it. "Wh-what do you want, Ian?" She hated herself for stuttering. Pressing her lips together, she promised herself she wouldn't do it again.

"Now, that's not much of a greeting," Ian said in his silky British accent. "But I suppose I deserve it."

"You deserve worse than that," Amy said.

"I know. I have done some terrible things to you. But we're in a contest. I learned from my father that the only important thing is to win," Ian said. "I hear his voice in my head all the time, like after a cricket match. *Ian, I don't care if you played well. Didn't you notice that your team lost? If you expect a pat on the back, you're not getting it from me!*"

Amy felt a spurt of sympathy. But Ian had manipulated her before. She wasn't going to fall for it again. No matter how sincere he sounded.

"Tell it to your therapist."

"Look, I deserve everything you're saying. I'm not

calling to gain your trust," Ian said. "I'm calling because I have some information."

"Tell it to someone who cares," Amy said. Dan moved closer so he could try to hear the other side of the conversation. Amy backed away. "Do you expect me to—"

"It's about your parents," Ian said. "About their death."

Amy froze.

"My mother told me everything. They were murdered."

Amy felt a buzzing in her ears. She couldn't concentrate. She just kept hearing the word *murdered*.

Parents . . . murdered . . . Parents . . . murdered . . .

"Amy?" She heard Ian talking, but she couldn't make sense of what he was saying.

Was it something she'd always known somehow? Deep down in a place she was afraid to look?

The fire . . . wet grass against her legs . . . Dan shivering in her lap . . . smoke and fire pouring out into the night air . . .

What was *that*? The image had just popped into her head. Amy put her fingers on her forehead and kneaded it, trying to make the image go away.

". . . wanted to talk to you about it. A temporary truce. We give you our word that nothing will happen. . . ."

Parents. Murdered.

"Will you come?" Ian asked.

"Tell me what you know." Amy struggled to keep her voice level. Her heartbeat pounded in her ears.

"This phone is not secure."

"What?"

"Trust me. It's not. Listen, I'll meet you in an open place with lots of people—The Rocks Market at Circular Quay. Meet me in front of the Museum of Contemporary Art at three o'clock."

Amy said nothing.

"I hope you do," Ian said, and hung up.

"So, what did the creep say?" Dan asked. "What did he expect you to do this time? No, don't tell me. You're going to fall for whatever he said, right? Oh, Ian," he said in a high voice, fluttering his eyelashes, "take me for a sail on your S.S. *Dreamboat* . . ."

Amy turned on him fiercely. "Cut it out, dweeb! He just asked for a meeting!"

"Stop the madness!" Dan said, holding his head and rocking back and forth. "My sister is a love alien!"

"DAN!"

"All right, you two," Nellie said. "Separate corners." She peered worriedly at Amy. "But you're not going to meet him, are you, Amy? Because . . ."

"I wish you two would stop treating me like I'm completely stupid," Amy said.

"Hey, if the Crocs fit," Dan muttered.

Amy jammed her hands in her pockets. She had to be alone and think. Because the idea was just too huge. She couldn't begin to talk about it. Not yet.

Parents. Murdered.

Amy turned and flung herself back into the house. Shep was just heading out, jingling his car keys. "Everybody ready to hit the road? We have time for a quick tour of Sydney, then let's head to the market for some grub."

"I'm going to hang out here," Amy said, trying to keep her voice calm. "Jet lag just hit. I need some downtime."

Nellie looked at her sympathetically. "You'll feel better after a nap."

"Are you going to dream about your dreamboat?" Dan asked.

"Down, boy," Nellie said to Dan. "Let's give Amy a rest."

They cleared out, and Amy was left alone with Ian's voice in her head. *Murder.* Was he lying? Or did he know who killed them?

Amy bent over and took deep breaths. Someone had killed her parents. Someone she probably even knew.

The Kabras couldn't be trusted.

She could be walking into a trap. She didn't care.

Because inside her brain one question burned: *Who?*

The late afternoon sun was still strong as she left the bus stop and walked toward the museum by the harbor. Circular Quay was a busy spot for tourists. She was relieved to find it crowded and lively. It was easy to lose herself in the wandering throngs. She stopped at the first store she found that sold touristy things and bought a baseball cap that read OZ. She pulled it low over her face as if she was shading her eyes from the bright afternoon sunlight.

She wished she could be one of the tourists with a camera, ambling through the maze of cobblestone streets and alleyways. This was one of the oldest parts of Sydney, and the stores and sidewalk cafés she passed looked tempting. Ahead, the spectacular Harbour Bridge curved against a brilliant bright blue sky. She caught her first glimpse of the famous Sydney Opera House, looking to her like a flower unfurling its petals. Music filled the air. Awnings mimicking the shape of the opera house roof shaded tables laden with crafts.

But she wasn't a tourist. Her strolling had a purpose. When she stopped to look in a store window, it wasn't to see the merchandise. It was to check out the people around her in the reflection. When she turned a corner and doubled back, it wasn't because she'd made a mistake in direction—it was to catch any tails behind her. And when she tilted her head to admire the surrounding buildings, she was checking out the rooflines and any possible flash from binoculars.

When Amy felt satisfied that she wasn't being followed, she headed down toward the museum. She slowed her steps and proceeded cautiously as she grew closer to the harbor. She was fifteen minutes ahead of schedule. Time to check out the area. She hung back in a doorway, watching the swirl of tourists. Every so often she checked her watch so that it would appear as though she was waiting for someone.

Suddenly, she felt someone behind her, a little too close.

"Beautiful day. Hope you are able to enjoy it."

Amy felt the fear curl inside her at the sound of that harsh Russian-accented voice. She tried to move away, but a group of tourists was directly in front of her, loudly discussing where to eat dinner. She felt something press against her back.

"By the way, the nails are loaded," Irina said.

All Irina had to do was bend back the joint of her finger, and a needle full of poison would sink into Amy's neck. She looked around frantically for a policeman.

"Do not be a stupid person. No one can help you. Now go."

She moved away from the harbor, back down the street. Her eyes searched the area, looking for a way out. Could she outrun Irina? Maybe. But Irina pressed so close behind her that Amy knew she'd never get away without a prick from that needle.

"Don't think. Just walk. No business that is funny. Now in here. Go." Irina urged her inside an old stone building. The door was unlocked, and she pushed it open. Irina crowded in behind her and shut the door.

They were in an old pub. The curved wooden bar stretched the length of the room. Dim light caught the flash of amber in bottles still lined up on a shelf. But cobwebs hung from the ceiling, and they had disturbed dust that swirled in the slanting sunlight.

"This way," Irina said, prodding Amy toward a small door at the back.

Fear coiled inside Amy. She had seen the blank, intense look in Irina's eyes in the Church on the Blood. Irina had been close to killing her and Dan that dark night. "No."

"Push door, please," Irina said. When Amy hesitated, Irina's foot shot forward and kicked open the door. She gave Amy a small shove. "If I were going to kill you, I could have done it ten times already. We need private talk away from the Kabras. When you don't show up on time, they'll come looking. So go."

Amy found herself in a large storeroom. Huge cans of baked beans and tomatoes sat on the shelves. "You've brought me to Costco?" she asked in a mocking voice. She needed to push back, let Irina know she wasn't paralyzed with fear. Even though she was.

"You should know by now I don't understand the jokes." Irina pushed her to the rear of the storeroom. A smaller door was set into the thick stone wall, made of old wood with deep, long cracks running down it. Irina produced a large iron key and fitted it into the lock. She pushed open the door. All Amy could see was darkness.

"Now I show you special piece of Australian history." Irina nudged her in the back. Amy felt the sharpness of her fingernail. "Go."

CHAPTER 8

A tiny penlight barely illuminated a rickety set of stairs. The door thudded shut behind them.

"We could meet an occasional rat," Irina said. "Otherwise, perfectly safe."

"Don't worry," Amy said. "I'm used to rats. They run in my family."

"Comedian like your brother, eh?" Irina said. "This tunnel was used in the 1800s. If a lowlife drank too much rum at a bar, he found himself on a ship out to sea the next morning. Smuggled through tunnel to harbor."

They reached the bottom of the stairs. The floor was dirt, the walls crumbling stone. Amy couldn't see what was ahead.

"Wh-where are you taking me?" She hated the quaver in her voice. She wouldn't let it out again.

"Ha!" Irina barked the word without humor. "You think I'm kidnapping you? I'm *saving* you. There are some things I won't stoop to do."

"Really," Amy said. "I thought you *stooped* at nothing."

"Is a joke? It's true, though, what you say. There was nothing I wouldn't do to win. But today, Amy Cahill, I'm doing you a favor. I'm giving you advice you need. Here it is—you are afraid of everything except what you should fear."

"Thanks," Amy said. "That was really helpful."

"For example, you are afraid of me right now. Understandable, I am your enemy. But at this moment, I am least of your problems."

"Really?" Amy said. "Weird. Seeing that I'm in a tunnel with rats, and you just threatened me with poison."

"Here is other thing I must tell you—you don't remember what you should never forget."

"That really clears up a lot."

"Go ahead, make the fun. But before we part, you must understand that what you don't know will doom you. And the world."

"Exaggerate much?" Somehow, taunting Irina kept her fear in check.

"No." Irina spun her around. In the darkness, she stood very close. "Listen to me, Amy Cahill. It is time you lift your head and look around you. The thirty-nine clues are like game to your brother, yes?"

Amy felt compelled by the ferocity of Irina's gaze. Her eyes, even in the faint glow of the penlight, were ice blue, her lashes startlingly dark against them. She couldn't deny what Irina had said. In many ways, the chase for the Clues *was* a game for Dan.

"But you know better. That's why I risk so much to talk to you. *Your parents died for this.* Do you think they wanted to go?"

"Don't talk about my parents!" Amy would have put her hands over her ears if she wasn't afraid it would make her look like a child.

"No parent would ever want to leave a child. Do you think they would leave their beloved children for a *game*?"

"Stop it!"

"Do you think your mother left you alone and raced back into a burning house just for her husband?"

Amy looked at Irina, startled. Frozen. "How do you know what happened?" she whispered.

Irina shrugged. "From newspaper, of course. Unless not. Only you know for sure. Because you know who was there that night. You were old enough to *see.* You won't believe what any Cahill tells you, and that is smart. We each have our agenda. So *you* must remember."

"I don't remember anything from that night," Amy said. But something dislodged and floated up into her brain, *cold grass, ash flying, a window shattering, Dan crying . . .*

"You have been resourceful, I give you that," Irina said. "You think on your feet, you and your brother. But there comes a time when you must think deeper. You must face the thing you don't want to face. Until you can do that, you're vulnerable."

"To what?"

"To someone who will tell you what you want to hear," Irina said. "So I ask again. What happened the night of the fire?"

She was choking through the cold, wet towel Mommy had placed over her mouth. Mommy held her hand so tightly. She could hear the flames, but she couldn't see them. It was all smoke. Dan cried in their mother's arms.

"I don't remember! I was a kid!" Fear tore the words from Amy's throat. The flashes she was getting were making her dizzy and sick.

"It's strange," Irina said, her gaze suddenly unfocused. "I remember so clearly being seven. The day I got separated from my mother on the streets of St. Petersburg . . . I remember the coat I was wearing, my shoes, the exact color of the river, the look on her face when she found me . . ."

"I'm happy for you," Amy said, swallowing hard.

"Did anyone visit the house that night?" Irina asked. "Did you hear anything? Did your mother come upstairs for you? How did you get out of the house?"

"Stop it!"

They fought their way down the stairs. Daddy was in the study, throwing books on the floor.

"Get the children out!" he shouted.

"Daddy!" she screamed. She held out her arms and he stopped for a second.

"Angel," he said, "go with Mommy."

"No!" She sobbed as her mother pulled her away. "No! Daddy!"

"No," Amy whispered. "No."

"We push away the bad memories," Irina said. Bleak sadness deadened her voice. "We tell ourselves is better not to remember. It is not better. Better to remember everything, even pain."

"What do you want from me?"

Irina's gaze snapped back into its glittering directness. "Come. We run out of time. This is a Lucian site. If we're both missing, it won't take long for Isabel to look here."

They started to walk again. Amy thought the light might have been getting grayer. Were they reaching the end of the tunnel? She was ready to run if they were. She felt something scurry past, and she jumped.

"Just a rat," Irina said. "One of the family, eh? And it's a rat who will fill your ears with lies."

"Stop!" Amy said. "If you're not going to kill me or kidnap me, the least you can do is talk straight."

They had reached the door. Amy saw the heavy iron lock. She wasn't getting out without Irina's help.

Irina stood with her back to the door. "Okay, I will talk straight. Isabel has called a meeting, yes?"

"Ian did."

Irina waved a hand dismissively. "Ian is the lure. She thinks you're stupid enough to come running if he asks. She chose him to dangle the bait. She knows you will come if you want to know who killed your parents."

"Does she know?"

Irina lifted a shoulder. "That is wrong question.

CAME

57

Right question is, will she tell you the truth? Of course not. She will tell you a lie in order to soften you. The lie will sound like truth. Then she will offer you a deal."

"And you think I'm dumb enough to believe what she tells me."

Irina held up a finger. "*Nyet,* not dumb. You are here with me now because I know you are smart. You need to know that if Isabel doesn't get her way, she can be . . . unreasonable. There will be bad consequences if you refuse the deal."

"So what do you want me to do?" Amy asked.

"Don't go. You don't need her version of that night. You have your own. Reach for it." Irina put her hand on the door. "This leads to the street three blocks from harbor. No surveillance here. You can catch bus or taxi right outside. Go back to wherever you are staying."

"Why should I?"

Irina sighed. "Because you must fear the right thing, as I said in beginning. Do you think whoever killed your parents would hesitate to kill you, too?"

"I don't believe anything that you're saying," Amy said. "I think you're trying to manipulate me and frighten me."

Irina's gaze flared in anger or exasperation, Amy couldn't tell which. "Little girl, keep up. You *should* be frightened." She hesitated. "What if I give you clue to let you know I'm telling the truth. Okay?"

"What's the catch?"

"No catch," Irina said impatiently. "Listen. Sooner

or later you will get hint leading you to New York City subway. The clue is hidden there in a mural in the tile. Seventeenth Street stop on number six subway train. I know what you will say—Irina, there is no stop on number six train for Seventeenth Street. But that is why the clue is so difficult to find. Rosemary. One sprig."

"Why should I believe you?"

Irina shrugged. "Thirty-nine clues, I give away one. So? As you would say, no biggie. It is worth it if you trust me."

"I could never trust you in a million years," Amy said.

"I'm not asking for a million years or never or for-ever," Irina snapped. "I'm asking for one day only. Today."

"Why are you doing this?" Amy asked. "If the clue is real, you just betrayed your branch."

Irina flinched. "I'm *doing* this for my branch. Someday I hope this becomes clear." She unlocked the door and pushed it open. "Turn right at end of alley. Go."

Amy's legs trembled as she walked out. She was in a dark, narrow alley. Ahead she could see sunlight and traffic, a taxi cruising by. When she reached the street, she looked behind her. Irina was gone.

Could Irina really have just let her go?

She hesitated. Why should she trust Irina? She was suddenly paralyzed with fear. Her parents had been murdered. This was all too real. Was someone watching her even now? If Irina had lied, she had also set a trap. If Amy hailed a taxi or got on a bus, someone would follow her straight to Shep's. Irina had said *wherever you are staying*. They still didn't know.

But if Irina *hadn't* lied, she was walking into Isabel's trap.

People were starting to look at her curiously. Did she look as stunned as she felt? She forced herself to move. When she reached the corner, she saw that she was now blocks away from the museum. A ferry was crossing the water, passing underneath the Harbour Bridge.

Maybe that could be her escape. Nobody expected her to leave by *water*.

She saw the ferry heading in. She was blocks from the museum. She could easily lose herself in the throng and jump aboard.

Legs pumping, Amy ran toward the ferry stop. Passengers filed down the gangway. She'd reach it in time.

She reached the dock and started down toward the ferry. Suddenly, a speedboat zipped in front of the idling ferry and came straight toward the dock. At the last moment, it cut its engine and the boat bobbed only inches away. A boy on the bow leaped down in front of her.

"There you are!" Ian said.

Isabel waved from the deck. "Amy! Come aboard!"

Amy glanced behind her. Irina stood at the end of the dock, blocking her way back to The Rocks. She was wearing sunglasses, and Amy couldn't read her expression.

Amy felt like a fool. Irina had planned this. She'd probably been behind her the whole way and radioed ahead to Isabel.

Ian slid an arm through hers. "I'm glad you came," he murmured. "There's a lot to say."

Isabel waved from the wheel of the boat. "Isn't it a beautiful day?"

Amy knew she had no choice. She had walked right into the trap. She shook off Ian's arm and climbed aboard.

CHAPTER 9

"Have a seat, Amy," Isabel said, pointing to the long cushioned bench in the stern of the speedboat. She was dressed casually in a striped T-shirt and trim white pants with white sneakers. "Let's take a quick tour of the harbor and then I'll show you the prettiest cove. I'll have you back in forty-five minutes. Promise!"

"I guess it's — " Amy's next words were drowned out as Isabel gunned the motor. The boat zipped away from the quay, passing right by the ferry as it blasted its horn. Amy clapped her hands over her ears.

"Oopsie, sorry!" Isabel laughed as she turned the wheel and skipped over another boat's wake. The waves thudded against the hull. "Let's get away from this traffic. Don't worry, Amy, I'm an expert captain."

"Mother keeps a boat at our place in the Bahamas," Ian shouted in Amy's ear. "She's raced competitively. There's no cause for concern."

In her head, she heard Dan mimicking Ian's British accent and formal words. She wished he was here to make fun of him. Anything to stop this dread in her stomach.

She had been afraid of grim, colorless Irina for so long and the menacing Holts that this new shape of villain didn't make sense. Isabel looked like a model. Her eyes sparkled and her smile was generous and warm. She was one of the most beautiful women Amy had ever seen. Isabel perched high on the captain's chair, her white sneaker swinging gaily. Dangerous? It didn't seem possible. Just another of Irina's lies.

An open path of water lay in front of them now. Amy's teeth slammed together as the boat surged forward. She felt the bow lift off the water. They raced across the harbor at what Amy considered a terrifying speed.

"That's more like it!" Isabel yelled. When she turned, her eyes were alight with excitement. "Don't you love it?"

"LOVE IT!" Ian shouted, but Amy noticed he was gripping the railing.

The boat slammed against the waves as they entered a rougher part of the harbor. Amy bounced up and down, trying to keep her seat. The wind whipped her hair into her eyes.

Finally, when Amy thought her bones might disintegrate into powder after being slammed against the water so much, Isabel cut the speed and motored into a beautiful cove. Amy saw a white horseshoe-shaped beach. She could see a sprinkling of people on the beach and a few swimmers beyond the surf line. She relaxed. She'd been afraid that Isabel would take her somewhere totally secluded or way out at sea. If she had to, she could dive off the boat and swim to shore from here.

The boat bobbed gently in the waves. Isabel crossed over and sat in a deck chair that faced Ian and Amy. She took each of their hands.

"Now, you two," she said. "Enough squabbling. You're here to make up."

Amy looked at her incredulously. *Squabbling?* Obviously, Mother Kabra didn't have a clue about the homicidal tendencies of her son.

Amy withdrew her hand. "I'm not here to make up with Ian," she said firmly. She was relieved that her voice came out so strong. "I'm here because he told me that my parents were murdered."

"Right to the point, aren't you?" Isabel dropped Ian's hand. "I admire that! All right, then. I'm going to tell you some things in confidence and hope that you will respect it. I didn't come to Australia just to collect my darling children." Isabel paused. "There is a mole in the Lucian branch. We believe this mole has been operating for some time. Thwarting us at every turn."

Nataliya, Amy thought. She had led Amy and Dan to Russia. She was a Lucian, but she'd helped them get their last Clue.

"We've wondered where they were getting information, resources. And then we realized. The Madrigals. One of our own has joined them."

Amy didn't believe it. If Isabel was talking about Nataliya, she had to be wrong. "What does this have to do with me?" Amy asked.

"I believe — *we* believe, those of us at the highest levels — that this person, this spy, this mole, along with the Madrigals — murdered your parents."

No. Isabel was definitely not talking about Nataliya. It was someone else. Nataliya had risked so much to help them.

"How do you know?" she asked, swallowing hard.

"The fire was deliberately set. Cleverly done," Isabel said. "We investigated ourselves. I'm sorry to shock you, Amy, but you must come to terms with it. You must see what you're up against. The Madrigals are ruthless."

"Why should I believe you?" Amy challenged. Why should she believe *anyone*?

Isabel's voice was soft. "Because I was close to your parents, for one thing. I mourned them. When I realized that the Lucian spy was aligned with the Madrigals, I decided I had to get involved with the hunt. I called off Ian and Natalie. I want an alliance with you and Dan. I will help you bring the murderer to justice."

"Who is it?" Amy asked, swallowing hard.

"Not only will I help you," Isabel said, ignoring Amy's question, "but the full resources of the Lucians will be placed before you and your brother. Information. Strongholds. Money. We'll share the clues, and we'll win together."

"Enough about the clues. *Who killed my parents?*"

"Irina Spasky."

The sun was sinking lower in the sky, staining the blue water with pink. The glare behind Isabel put her face in shadow, obliterating her features. It seemed to flare out like fire around her. Amy felt dizzy.

This was what Irina had warned her about. *The lie will sound like truth.* But was it a lie? Or did Irina just want her to think it was?

"My husband and I knew Irina when we were all teenagers," Isabel said. "I watched her turn from an idealistic scholar into a cold-blooded killer. But I never dreamed she'd strike against her own relatives. The chase for the clues is a hunger for her. It's warped her. I'm sorry, Amy. This can't be easy to hear. But you should know who killed them."

And Isabel *did* look sorry. Her bright eyes, the color of dark honey, were full of sympathy.

"If we join forces, we can defeat her," Isabel said. "We can *expose* her. That's what she fears more than anything. The Madrigals . . . they are the game changers. What do we know about them? Only that they're bent on the destruction of all Cahill branches . . . and yet nobody knows who or what they are. We suspect that the group was formed by rogue Cahills hundreds of years ago, and they are committed to the destruction of the entire family. Surely you'd think the branches would unite against them. But for all those years, the branches couldn't form an alliance, even against a common enemy. Until now." Isabel clasped her hands. "We can make the future, Amy. We can find the thirty-nine clues and you can avenge your parents. If we work together."

"I don't see what you get out of this," Amy said.

"Your brains. Your brother's instincts. You have to admit you've bested even my own children. And remember this, Amy—you could already *be* a Lucian. Grace chose not to have allegiances. You seem most like a Lucian to me," Isabel said. Her voice was husky, warm. She opened her arms. "So this could be just . . . coming home. One more thing we offer, the most important thing. Protection. Irina has more tricks up her sleeve, I promise you. And the Madrigals are ruthless."

Had she been in the tunnel with her parents' murderer? Amy thought again of the look in Irina's eyes at the confrontation in the church crypt. She knew Irina was capable of terrible things. . . .

Unless . . . Irina had told the truth, and it was Isabel who was lying. Amy felt her stomach churn.

Trust no one, Mr. McIntyre had said. For the first time, she truly understood what he meant. The stakes were so much higher than she'd thought. The lies cut so much deeper. Right to her heart.

"What do you say, Amy?" Isabel looked at her with concern. "I hate to hit you with this all at once, but you need to get up to speed, and fast, if you want to survive."

Why would Isabel just *assume* Amy would believe her? Because Ian had duped her so easily? She looked over at him. He was gazing at his mother, his handsome

IN TOO DEEP

profile turned to Amy. He had barely said a word on the boat. He hadn't even met her gaze, not once.

He had lied to her over and over again. Had he told his mother how gullible Amy was?

It didn't matter, Amy thought. If it was the truth, then she and Dan would figure out what to do about it. Together. They were a team. They'd gotten this far.

She lifted her chin. "Dan and I can handle our own problems. So thanks, but no thanks."

A tiny flush stained Isabel's cheek. Amy noted some perspiration above her lip. "You need to be certain," Isabel said tightly. "I can't make this offer again."

"It's my final answer," Amy said.

Isabel paused just a fraction of a moment. Then she smiled. "I understand. I'll take you back."

She stood and went to the railing. "But first, let's take a moment to admire this lovely cove. Australia has the most beautiful beaches in the world, don't you agree? Of course, you have to watch out for riptides and bluebottles and sharks, but what are the odds of them finding you? Shark attacks are actually quite rare. I find sharks beautiful. The great white is a machine that searches for food constantly. It has one purpose in life, and it knows exactly what it is and what to do about it. It can rip your arm or your leg off with one bite, but you can't blame the shark. And then when blood foams in the water, what else can it do but keep feeding?"

"Mum, please—" Ian started to say, but Isabel just talked over him.

"Have you ever been in a shark cage? I have. I've looked into a shark's eyes and it's like looking at death itself."

Isabel walked over to a storage compartment on the far side of the deck. She flipped open the top and hoisted out a large white bucket. Amy saw the muscles in her arms flex as she lifted it and carried it over to the railing. She reached in and began to ladle something into the water.

The smell reached Amy's nose just as the realization hit. Isabel was tossing fish parts into the water. Amy saw the slimy white chunks, the bloody ends. She heard the *splash* as half of a bloody fish hit the water.

She felt Ian tense up next to her. His hands gripped the edge of the seat cushion.

Isabel didn't look at Amy. She was smiling to herself as she ladled out the macabre stew.

Amy looked out over the calm blue water. She saw the fin. It moved back and forth in a line a few yards from the boat. She saw another, farther out. The sharks must have smelled the blood. Now they were tacking back and forth, heading for the boat.

Isabel straightened. She went over to a shelf by the wheel and pumped out a dollop of antibacterial gel on her hands. She rubbed them together briskly.

"All right, then," she said brightly. "Why don't you tell me all the clues that you and your brother have gathered? Or would you rather go for a swim?"

CHAPTER 10

There was no hint of cruelty on Isabel's face. That was the scariest thing of all. Just that same bright smile.

"Are you out of your mind?" Amy asked.

But Isabel didn't seem crazy. Now Amy could see the ice under the warmth. "You don't need a suit," Isabel said. "It won't matter in a few seconds anyway. Or minutes. The sharks might be feeding on the fish parts, but they'll get to you eventually." She kicked the bucket slightly with her bright white sneaker. "And I have plenty more. So. What do you say? Swim or talk?"

"I'm not jumping in that water," Amy said, standing up and going to the opposite side of the boat.

"Well, if you won't do it yourself, I can toss you in," Isabel said. "Heave ho and all that. Martial arts training. Not a problem. Ian can help."

"Mum?" Ian's voice wobbled a bit.

She turned on him fiercely. Her voice was like a knife cutting glass. "Not *Mum*! How many times must I remind you? It makes me sound old!" She regained her composure and shrugged at Amy. "So, maybe my lazy *coward* of a son won't give me a hand. But I don't need one."

She moved toward Amy. Amy backed away until she hit the rail. There was nowhere to go except the water.

"Little Amy and little Dan," she said. "Who knew they would find a way to travel the world? Paris, Moscow, Venice, Seoul, Karachi. You sent the Lucian stronghold into a frenzy."

Karachi? Amy thought through her panic. She and Dan hadn't been to Karachi.

"Who helped you in Russia? How many clues have you found?" Isabel planted her muscled arms on the rail on either side of Amy. Up close, Amy could see the eerie tight perfection of her skin, the cruel glow in her dark golden eyes.

"Throw some more fish in the water," Isabel barked to Ian.

Ian didn't move.

"NOW!"

Ian rose and went toward the bucket. Amy's heart banged against her chest, and she couldn't seem to get a breath. Isabel was no longer pinning her against the rail, but she was close and ready to spring. Amy wondered what her chances were if she ran to the bow and jumped in. If she swam as fast as she could, how far could she make it before a shark chewed off a piece of her?

Isabel turned impatiently to watch Ian, and Amy saw something out of the corner of her eye. A spray of bright colors in the sky over Isabel's shoulder. Orange, purple, pink—striped paragliders soaring over the beach.

The red-and-orange paraglider moved faster than the rest. It scudded across the sky, making a wide loop over the water. Amy realized that it was catching wind currents, heading closer and closer to the boat. She saw a pair of beefy white legs dangling. Meaty hands on the controls.

Hamilton!

Not by a flicker, not by a breath, did Amy indicate what she saw bearing down on them. Isabel urged Ian to hurry. The shark fins circled the boat.

Amy tensed as Hamilton caught a downdraft. He temporarily blocked out the sun. Isabel looked up, shading her eyes, as he zoomed down. "Come on!" he shouted to Amy. She leaped up on the cushioned bench and grabbed for his ankles.

"Woo-hoo!" Hamilton screamed as Amy tucked up her legs and held on.

Isabel screamed in fury and tried to grab Amy's legs. Hamilton steered the paraglider away. It lurched to the left, and Isabel sprang and snatched at empty air. At the same time, Amy kicked savagely at the bucket. It tipped, spilling fish guts and blood over the deck. Isabel slipped and fell into it. Blood and guts stained her pristine sneakers and white pants. She screamed.

"Way to go, Amy!" Hamilton chortled.

But another gust of wind sent them scudding sideways, and Isabel managed to grab hold of Amy's ankle with a bloody, fishy hand. Amy screamed and kicked.

"Whoa!" Hamilton shouted as the paraglider tilted.

Isabel slipped and fell back into the fish parts. Amy tucked up her legs again as they sailed over the boat railing. She was barely clearing the water now. Only inches below the surface she could see the dark mass of the shark.

"H-Hamilton . . ."

"Just hang on!" he shouted.

Amy's sneaker skidded along the surface. The shark whipped around.

"HAMILTON!"

"Don't worry! This baby has a motor!"

"Then USE IT!"

The motor kicked on. The paraglider rose inches above the water. They skimmed along, and it rose higher and higher. Soon they were soaring over the bay.

"Okay!" Hamilton yelled. "I think I have the hang of it now. . . ."

Amy's arms began to ache. "Hamilton, I can't hold on!" she shouted. If she fell from this height, she didn't think she would make it.

"No problemo, Ame-o," Hamilton called. With his powerful legs, he simply bent his knees and pulled her up higher. "Grab on to the harness," he told her. Amy grabbed the paraglider bar, and they lurched to the side. "Whoa, baby," Hamilton said to the paraglider, correcting the movement.

"That was a little too close," Hamilton said. "Sorry. This is my first time on one of these things."

"And you flew down to rescue me? Weren't you scared?"

"Holts don't feel fear," Hamilton said. "Haven't you heard?"

The other paragliders were soaring toward them now. She saw Eisenhower's red face. He was shouting something.

"What is your dad saying?" Amy asked.

"Don't know," Hamilton said. "I turned off my radio. He probably wants me to land so we can question you. He has no idea why you're in Australia. It's driving him bonkerinos. But you came through and gave me that clue. So I owe you."

He soared to the far end of the beach, coming in near the shallow water. "There's a road at the end of the beach," he told her. "You can find your way back."

"Looks like I owe *you* one now," Amy said.

"You bet. I'll collect one day. Don't forget the Hammer. The Holt brigade is behind that hill, so they won't see you if you run fast. Keep your knees bent when you jump and run like a hurricane wind. I'm going to take off again."

He gently steered the paraglider down. "Now!" he yelled, and Amy let go.

She bent her knees as she hit the soft sand and took off. Hamilton rose, catching an updraft, and was soon sailing high above her.

Her legs were shaking, but she managed to run up to the road. She slowed to a walk when she knew she was safe. She tried not to think about the sharks and the bloody water.

Jamming her trembling hands into her pockets, she started to walk. Images bombarded her—fire, blood, sharks, Isabel's lipsticked mouth like a scar. The sun around Isabel's head had looked like fire. . . .

Damp grass against her bare legs. Smoke. Fire. Her mother bending over her, her hands on Amy's cheeks . . .

Amy shook her head hard. She didn't have to remember! She didn't *want* to! The images made her feel sick and dizzy and scared.

You don't remember what you should never forget.

But what if she didn't *want* to remember? What if she wanted to lock away a memory forever?

CHAPTER 11

Mummy wasn't happy.

That was never good.

But this time, it was sour-faced Spasky getting the heat. *That* was sweet.

Natalie kept her posture straight, even though it was difficult on the cushy sofa. She kept sliding forward on the slippery satin. But even while Mummy ranted, she could spot slumping shoulders.

Ian sat next to her. He'd come back seasick, his face the color of her new chartreuse Prada purse.

"This is your fault." Isabel's voice had taken on the cool, precise tone that Ian and Natalie privately called *the scalpel*. It sliced you open and left you bleeding. She paced in front of Irina, her high heels making dents in the thick carpet of the hotel suite. Her heavy charm bracelet jangled along with her agitation. "I had to soak for an *hour* to get the smell out. I had to throw away my entire outfit. And it was Chanel!"

Natalie shuddered. Nothing worse than losing couture.

"Not to mention that the girl got away!" Isabel put her hand to her throat, where Amy's jade necklace gleamed against her sleeveless white dress. Natalie had no idea why she was wearing it when she could be wearing diamonds.

"Excuse me, but I don't see why this is my fault," Irina said. "Reminder: I was not on boat."

Ian stiffened beside her and Natalie stared at Irina, fascinated. Didn't she have any idea how to handle Isabel when she was angry? You had to agree with everything she said and apologize, no matter how unfair the accusations were. Otherwise, you were toast.

Isabel wheeled and approached her. Natalie knew that look. Irina was about to get it. Both barrels between the eyes. This was going to be very good.

"Excuse *me*," Isabel said witheringly. "You had one simple assignment. Find Amy. Bring her to the boat."

"Excuse me for second time," Irina said. "She did go aboard boat, which was the objective. I do not see—"

"You do not see because you are a fool!" Isabel let her contempt drip from every word. "You were supposed to deliver Amy at three-twelve *exactly*. And you were supposed to arrive by Argyle Street so that Ian could spot you with the binoculars and I could prepare the boat. You didn't do any of it! You were fifteen minutes late. Fifteen minutes! That gave the Holts enough time to get organized. Even those thick skulls don't need too long to figure out a plan!" Isabel planted herself in front of Irina. "They had us under surveillance.

And you are responsible for *counter*surveillance. So add it up, Irina. Not only did you fail . . . you failed *miserably.*"

Natalie smirked. Why shouldn't she let Irina know how much she was enjoying this? Irina had never gotten it into her head that she wasn't the boss. Ian and Natalie were the personal representatives of Vikram and Isabel. They were the *de facto* Lucian leaders. Irina couldn't bear that.

Isabel held up her thumb and index finger a fraction apart. "I was this close to getting her to tell all the clues they had. This close! That little mouse was terrified."

"What if she didn't?" Irina asked.

"What if she didn't what?"

"Cooperate. You would throw her to sharks?"

"Don't bore me with what ifs," Isabel said, turning and waving a hand. "I am about *results.* And now we've been defeated. By the *Tomas.* Unacceptable!"

Isabel's narrow, toned shoulders lifted up, then down. When she turned around, her expression was calm. Not that her face ever showed much emotion. Isabel kept the best plastic surgeons in London very busy. She'd been pulled, pricked, smoothed, and plumped. Natalie wished her mother wasn't *quite* so obsessed, but she guessed that once you were in your forties, it was a gigantic amount of work to keep yourself up.

"The thing is, Irina, this isn't the first time you've

failed to achieve our objectives," she said. "You're slipping. You're . . . well, frankly, you're *old*."

"Reminder," Irina said. "We are the same age."

"Old *thinking*," Isabel said. "You don't keep up. You were once the best spy in the business. I give you that. But if you don't shape up, you're going to be out. Do you understand? It's crunch time, as the Americans say. There is no such thing as failure for a Kabra."

"Don't you mean, no such thing as failure for the Lucians?" Irina asked.

Isabel looked uncertain for a moment. "Of course that is what I meant."

"Because this contest is about power for the Lucian Cahills, not the Kabra family," Irina said. "Unless I've been misinformed."

"Well, naturally." Isabel's fingers drummed on her leg.

Somehow, Irina had succeeded in making Mummy uncomfortable. Isabel flicked a piece of lint off her dress as though it were a missile. Natalie hoped her mother would demolish Irina, or they'd be in for a very bad afternoon.

"And I would also argue that perhaps Kabras do know failure occasionally," Irina continued, keeping her voice bland. "Your children, for example."

You hateful witch, Natalie thought. She waited for Ian to say something, but he was like a statue next to her.

Irina smiled. "It seems that Amy and Dan Cahill have bested them at every turn. How many clues have you two collected?" she asked. "I mean, the two of you, alone. How many?" She put a finger to her temple. "Let me think . . . oh, I remember! One."

"Mummy!" Natalie half rose. "She can't talk to us that way!"

Irina turned back to Isabel. "The truth is that those two have turned out to be much smarter than we expected. And what if they discover what really happened to their parents? Now, they are resourceful. If they have an even greater reason to win—revenge—they will be *dangerous*."

Suddenly, Isabel undid the clasp of the jade necklace and threw it at Irina's feet.

"*That* is what I think of those Cahills. Not to mention your ridiculous obsession with Grace Cahill. She was a batty old lady who thought she knew best. Well, she and her grandchildren won't get in our way—no matter how much they know."

Irina picked up the necklace. She ran her fingers along the carved dragon in the center.

"You thought it was important," Isabel said. "Another one of your mistakes. I had it thoroughly checked this morning. It's just a necklace. A cheap piece of sentimentality that the girl clings to. It was a waste of my time to steal it. Well, I'm done wasting time. Now, if you could manage to do one simple thing." Isabel tossed her cell phone to Irina. "Call the Fixer."

Who's the Fixer? Natalie wondered.

Irina cleared her throat. "I am no longer sure of his reliability."

"Of course he's reliable," Isabel countered. "We've used him many times. Tell him I'm in Sydney and I need a few things. I'll contact him later with a list."

Isabel picked up her purse. "Ian, Natalie. Come. We're going shopping."

Natalie popped up. At last!

"Let yourself out, Irina."

The door slammed behind them. Natalie had to practically skip to keep up with her mother's fast pace. "Irina is just jealous of you," she said. "She wants to be leader, and she's just hopeless at it."

"Right," Ian said. Natalie shot him a look. He was supposed to sound *enthusiastic*. Isabel counted on them for support.

She expected her mother to smile and agree, but Isabel just stabbed the elevator button. "Shut up, Natalie, I'm trying to think," she snapped.

Natalie rubbed her fingers along the fabric of her sweater. Cashmere. Her mother had bought her one in every color. Whenever she felt upset, she thought of them stacked in her huge closet at home in London. She had the best mother in the world.

Isabel stabbed the elevator button again. "Call the concierge, Ian," she barked. "First, order a car. And second, tell them to fix their elevators."

"Yes, Mummy."

"And don't speak to me, either of you," Isabel said as the elevator doors opened. "I have to think."

CHAPTER 12

The echo of the door slam faded. Irina stared at the phone. She would have to call the Fixer. He could be out of the country on a job, but that would be too much to hope for.

There was one in every city, she supposed, a person who could get anything you needed. Passports, cars, explosives, poisons. The Lucians found such contacts valuable. The Fixer was one of the best. He did not balk at anything, he could get anything, and he asked no questions. She had used him herself.

What would Isabel need from him this time? What was she planning?

Restlessly, Irina paced the room. She had lost Isabel's confidence. She no longer knew the plan, only parts of it.

She ran her fingers over the cool green stones of the necklace. Isabel's insults had washed over her like water. They hadn't stung.

She slid the necklace into the pocket of her black jacket and zipped the pocket shut. She never felt sentimental. Ever. Yet she understood sentiment. Having something a loved one had touched. Keeping it near.

When she had finally made herself clean out Nikolai's room all those years ago, she had folded his favorite pair of pants and found something in the pocket. Her own school medal for First Place Vaulting Championship. The metal was tarnished, the ribbon tattered and faded. But Nikolai had carried it with him. He had touched it every day. A reminder of his mother. She was away so much. He needed something real to keep her with him. She hadn't known.

She hadn't known.

That had been the moment she had broken. She had held the pants against herself and sobbed. She had screamed out her agony. She had put herself back together slowly, but she was never the same. She was still broken. She had lost her son.

She slid her hand into her other pocket and touched the medal. Now it was her turn to keep something close as a reminder. To touch something he had touched.

Irina, the problem in Helsinki needs your attention.

My son is sick. It's not a good time.

She still remembered Isabel's brittle laugh.

Children are sick all the time.

No, it is more than that. The doctor said . . .

Don't bore me with details. Do your job. The tickets are waiting for you at the airport.

So she had kissed him, kissed his golden curls. She had whispered that she would be gone for only two days. Anna, her neighbor who watched him, whom he adored, Anna would be by his side. Irina would bring him back anything he wanted.

A monkey, he said, and she had laughed.

She had to go undercover. No communication, no phones, nothing. So she did not collect Anna's increasingly frantic messages. She did not get the doctor's call. She touched down in Moscow two days later and discovered that her nine-year-old son was dead. She was holding the stuffed monkey, an expectant smile on her face, when a weeping Anna told her the news.

Now Irina rose. Once Isabel had forced her to do something that she regretted with every waking breath. It would not happen again.

CHAPTER 13

The delicious smells of good things cooking greeted Amy as she wearily pushed open the door to Shep's house. It had taken her over an hour to get back. Plenty of time for her to digest what had happened. But it still hadn't taken away her fear. It was still there in her stomach, a cold, hard ball.

When she closed the door, she began to shake. Now that she was safe, the horror of what had happened truly sank in. What if Hamilton hadn't saved her? She saw herself falling into that water, saw the sharks circling with their dead black eyes. . . .

She felt so cold. She couldn't take a step, she was shaking so hard.

In the kitchen area, Nellie was cooking, a bright bandanna wrapped around her hair. She stirred something in a pan while outside Shep tended to the barbecue. Dan was playing one-person Foosball, running back and forth to each end of the table.

Nellie looked up. Her welcoming smile faded as she took in Amy's appearance.

She dropped the wooden spoon, splattering tomato sauce on the stove. Amy saw it bloom like blood in the water. Dizziness swept over her, a buzzing in her ears. The room started to spin. . . .

Nellie caught her as her knees gave way.

"Dan, get a blanket!" Nellie's voice was steady, but it rang through the open space. She half carried Amy to the couch.

The only thing Dan could find was the leather jacket. He brought it over and Amy gratefully wrapped herself in it.

"What happened?" Dan asked, his small face looking pinched. She'd spooked him.

"They didn't hurt me. I mean, if I'd been thrown into the bloody fish water with the sharks, who knows? But Hamilton came by on a paraglider, so—"

"What?" Nellie exclaimed at the same moment that Dan yelled, "Sharks?"

Quickly, Amy recounted how Irina had led her through the tunnel and warned her about Isabel, yet she'd wound up on the boat anyway. She explained how Isabel had offered them Lucian protection and what had happened when she'd said no. When she described Isabel calmly ladling the fish parts into the sea, Nellie turned white. But the funny thing was that as Amy told the story, she stopped shaking, and her fear went away.

She told them everything, including the rosemary Clue that Irina had given her. But she didn't tell them the most important thing. That Ian, Irina, and Isabel all told her that Hope and Arthur had been murdered. And that Isabel had accused the Madrigals and Irina of the crime.

"Oh, man," Dan said, throwing himself back on the cushions. "I missed it! If I'd been there, Isabel Cobra wouldn't have had a chance. We could have pushed *her* into the water. Or I could have gotten fishing line and tied her up. Or we could have used Ian as a battering ram!"

"Dan," Nellie chided. "This isn't a game."

The thirty-nine clues are like game to your brother, yes?

Dan jumped up and began pretending to paraglide over snapping sharks. Amy made a decision as she watched him. She couldn't tell him about their parents. There was a soft, secret spot in her brother that he covered up with jokes. It was all about losing his parents so young—before he could even have memories of them. She would have to try to figure it out on her own. At least for awhile.

Amy touched her throat, momentarily forgetting that Grace's necklace was gone. The absence of it made her feel more alone than ever. This feeling inside—that there was something she needed to remember—was big and scary. She'd have to hide that from Dan, too.

He hates when I act like a big sister. But I am one.

Nellie patted her knee. "Food. That's what you need." She got up and went back to the kitchen.

Amy wrapped the jacket more tightly around herself. She felt the lining tear and she groaned softly. The only thing she had from her mother, and she'd ripped it! She moved her fingers along the lining, searching for the tear, and heard something crackle. Sitting up, she examined it more closely. The jacket had already been torn along the seam and repaired again. She reached inside the tear and took out a brittle piece of lined paper—something ripped from a notebook.

"What is it?" Dan asked, coming closer.

"A piece of old notebook paper hidden in the lining." Her heart pounding, Amy read the words aloud.

28 June 1937

Each stronghold I was able to enter seems shaky now. War is on the horizon, nothing seems simple or safe, from Natal to Karachi. They fear us; that is good.

Left Bandung and flew to Darwin. Here we sent back parachutes to lighten load so I am including this jacket as well. GP has been instructed to pass it along to you. Tomorrow we go on to Lae. Then it is off across the Pacific to Howland.

I'm sorry to report that I failed to find our assassin H, or any real clues to his whereabouts. I was able to get to Batavia from Bandung and managed to find our contact. He told of a "scarred white man" who the natives believed had escaped the mountain. His body was intact but not his mind. What he had endured was terrible enough to break it.

Here in Darwin our informer turned out to be a dead end. It was soon clear that the gentleman—and I use the term loosely, because he was quite a charlatan—was just looking for another payoff. All he offered was riddles. He even had the audacity to try to sell me a ring—it will bring you luck, he said, so I bought it in hopes it would gain me information. It didn't. When I asked again if he knew H, he said both of them were in a hole but not to worry. Then he cackled a laugh and that was the end of it. Clearly he enjoyed giving me no information . . . and making me pay for it.

I am off into the blue. No more strongholds to penetrate. Only sky. AE

"I don't get it," Dan said. "Who do you think AE is? Some Australian dude who flew a plane?"

"Not a dude," Amy said with dawning excitement.

She sprang up and ran to Shep's bookshelves. Naturally, she'd already checked out his library. Shep had whole shelves dedicated to aviation history. It didn't take long before she found what she was looking for. She thumped the book down on the surfboard table.

Dan hurried over. "Amelia Earhart?"

"It's got to be!" Amy said. "Her last flight was right around that time." One of Amy's childhood heroes had been Amelia Earhart. Grace had given her a biography of the flier when she was eight years old. "She was amazing. She was the first woman to fly solo over the Atlantic. She broke records for speed and altitude. She didn't let anything stop her."

She flipped to the index and looked up "last flight." Then she turned to the page and read through the itinerary. "Look," she said, pointing to the page. "She was in Darwin, Australia, on June 28, 1937. She was trying to become the first woman to circumnavigate the world, and by the longest distance. And Dan, look at the rest of her stops!" She placed the paper with her parents' itinerary next to Amelia's journey. Her parents had hit many of the major stops.

"They match," Dan said. "But why would Mom and Dad be following where Amelia Earhart went about a bazillion years before?"

"About sixty years before," Amy corrected. She tapped the paper. "Isabel said something to me about the Lucian stronghold in Karachi. I bet all these cities are strongholds for other branches, too."

"So what happened after she left Darwin?"

"She flew to Lae, New Guinea, for refueling. Then she took off for Howland Island—which is basically a speck in the middle of the Pacific—but she never made it. Her plane was never found. There were all sorts of rumors that she survived, but basically everyone believes that she and her navigator couldn't locate the island and ran out of gas. But *before* that happened, it looks like she had a secret agenda. Do you realize what this means? She was a Cahill!"

"So who was GP?" Dan asked.

Amy searched through the book. "It must be George Putnam, her husband. They shipped the parachutes back because they would be useless over water. But whoever she trusted to ship the jacket didn't do it. Even then, it would have been valuable as a souvenir. It must have just stayed in Darwin. Mom must have had some kind of lead to it. . . ."

"'Our assassin H,'" Dan read. "Do you think it could be Bob Troppo? Maybe she's using the word *assassin* in a funny way because he hit Mark Twain with his cane. She says he has scars, just like the photograph."

"It has to be!" Amy said. "The Cahills have been looking for him for a long time, I guess. I wonder why." She reread the letter. "I wonder where Bandung is."

Shep overheard her from the kitchen, where he was transferring grilled fish onto a platter. "It's on the island of Java, not far from Jakarta," he said. "Indonesia."

"It was Earhart's stop before she flew to Darwin," Amy said.

"'They fear us,'" Dan read. "Who is 'they'?"

Amy looked up and met his gaze. "Who does every branch fear?"

"Madrigals," Dan said.

"Isabel said that Madrigals might be rogue Cahills—they left their own branches and formed a new group. They're like a secret society. That would explain why nobody really knows who they are. . . . They're just afraid of them." Amy frowned. "But Amelia Earhart couldn't be a Madrigal. She just couldn't. She was a hero. An explorer. And not only that, she wasn't . . . sneaky or mean. I can't believe she'd betray her branch just to get power." *Or that she could belong to a group that would one day kill our parents . . . if that part of the story is even true.*

"Maybe she was just really good at hiding things," Dan said, frowning. "Okay, we've got Amelia Earhart, branch strongholds, and some crazy dude with no name—maybe he's H, maybe he's Bob, but he's definitely a few Lucky Charms short of a bowl," Dan summarized. "I *still* don't know what we're doing in Australia. And what were our parents doing here? And why did they come to Sydney? Amelia Earhart didn't."

"Well, they probably flew here so that they could meet up with Shep and have him take them on his own plane. Less chance to be followed that way."

Amy turned back to Shep and raised her voice. "Shep, why did our parents go to Adelaide? Do you know?"

"Sure," Shep said. "We needed a refueling stop before Darwin. We had a couple of choices, and they picked Adelaide."

He put down the platter of fish on the dining table.

"I don't want to be nosy," he said, "but I have a feeling I don't have the whole story here. So far today we've been attacked by very large American surfers, Amy disappears for hours and then shows up looking like death warmed up, and now apparently Amelia Earhart is speaking to you from a watery grave. Do you want to fill me in on what's going on? Since I'm flying you over half of Australia and I happen to be your cousin, I think I have a right to know."

"Absolutely," Dan said. "The truth is that we're part of a gang of master thieves who broke into the US Mint and stole one billion dollars in gold. Amy and I are small enough to climb into AC ducts. We took off with the gold, so they're chasing us. But what they don't know is that we're working directly for the president."

"And Amelia Earhart . . ."

". . . was on a secret mission to find a place to hide the world's gold in a top secret underwater fortress. We're looking for that, too."

Shep nodded. "O-kay. Glad we got that straightened out. Now it's time to eat."

Amy couldn't sleep. Every time she closed her eyes she saw Irina's fierce gaze, blue as a flame in the darkness.

Do you think your mother left you alone and raced back into a burning house just for her husband?

Remember that night, Amy. Think about that night. You were there. You were old enough to see.

All this confusion, all this tightness in her chest made her feel like she couldn't breathe. Why was she so afraid? Why did Isabel seem so familiar to her, and why did that fill her with dread?

Nellie snoozed next to her, and Dan was just a lump wrapped in a quilt on the sofa by the window. Amy slipped out of bed. The leather jacket was lying on the armchair near Dan, and she put it on and wrapped it around her. The thrilling thought that it had belonged to Amelia Earhart had been replaced by the simple need to touch something her mother had touched. She lay her cheek against the collar.

"I miss them." Dan's voice was sleepy. "How can you miss people you can't remember?"

"I miss them, too," Amy said softly. "Being here is so weird. Because they were here, too."

"Yeah. It feels like they could just walk in the door any second. I don't know why."

Amy realized that she felt the same way. She felt closer to her parents here. Closer than she'd felt in a long time. And they were half a world away from everything they knew.

Dan yawned. "They left us for a whole month." His voice was drowsy, and she could tell he was close to sleep. "That's a long time to leave your kids."

"It must have been super important," Amy whispered.

"I'm glad they were searching for the clues, just like us," Dan said. He yawned again. "Wouldn't it be great if after this is over . . . Shep could maybe be our dad? We could move in with him. . . ."

"Dan, I don't know. He's not the dad type."

"People don't know they're the dad type until they're dads. Besides, can you imagine going back to Beatrice the Bloody?"

Amy couldn't. She couldn't imagine what the end of this would be like at all. But as soon as Dan said it, she realized he was right. She *couldn't* imagine going back to Aunt Beatrice. She couldn't imagine going back to school, or Boston.

They didn't belong there anymore.

They didn't belong anywhere.

After a minute, Dan's breathing was deep and regular. Amy went back to the foldout couch she shared with Nellie. She climbed back under the covers and she fell asleep, clutching her mother's jacket around her.

She dreamed. Her mother's hand gripping hers. A fire crackling in the fireplace. And then a fire out of control . . . ash falling like snow on the lawn.

"Get the children out!"

She woke with a start. It was still dark. She could hear Nellie's soft breathing next to her.

And then memory lit up her brain, and the shadows went away.

She hadn't gone to sleep after her bath. She'd turned

on her little green glass lamp and picked out a book. Sometimes she read herself to sleep. It was a secret she kept from her parents. Grace knew. Grace always let her.

So she heard the sound of visitors arriving. Heard a murmur of voices. Then suddenly the voices were raised. She got up and listened. She was dressed in her nightgown, the one with the koalas her mother had brought back from her long trip. Her parents' voices sounded different. There was something hard in their voices, something that glinted and clanked like coins.

She crept down the stairs and then down the hall to her father's study. She couldn't see her parents. Strangers surrounded them. The lights were low, but the fire blazed in the hearth.

She heard bursts of words, and Amy closed her eyes, trying to remember.

The violation of the strongholds . . .

Where did you go . . .

And her father's voice: Our travels are our business, not yours.

Let's all calm down. We only want what is ours.

Where did you go . . .

Tell us or . . .

Or what? You are standing in my home and you dare to threaten me?

Her mother's voice was hard and cool. It scared Amy. She burst through the circle. "Mommy!"

But before her mother could scoop her up, someone else did. Someone who smelled of perfume and makeup. A beautiful lady with big eyes the color of honey. In Amy's mind, she'd seen the flicker of fire reflected there.

"And who is this? What a pretty nightgown! Such cheerful teddy bears."

"Koalas," Amy corrects, because she's proud to know the word.

The lady's fingers tighten, just a bit. She looks over Amy's head and smiles at Mommy and Daddy.

"Did your mommy and daddy bring it back for you from their trip?"

The lady holds her too tightly. Amy starts to squirm, but the grip doesn't loosen.

And her mother looks so afraid . . .

Amy sat up in bed. The truth brought a rush of horror. The facts pounded her like body blows.

The lady holding her had been Isabel Kabra. Who else was there? She strained to remember. A bunch of people, strangers to her at the time. She'd been too shy to look at their faces. They knew her parents had come back from a trip but they weren't sure where they'd gone. For some reason, they had to know. Her parents had hidden the destination from them . . . until a seven-year-old girl had run downstairs in her nightgown and said the word *koalas.*

And then her parents' enemies had their answer.

She had betrayed them.

CHAPTER 14

"Rise and shine, mates," Shep called cheerfully. "I'm going to make a pot of coffee and a bit of brekkie, and then we're off to the field. Everybody sleep okay?"

It was still dark out. Shep had switched on the lights.

"*Mmmfff,*" Nellie said, her head in the pillow.

"Great," Dan said, sitting up in a tangle of quilts.

While Nellie put the pillow over her head and Shep started the coffee, Amy rose woodenly and went to the bathroom. She splashed cold water on her face and looked at herself in the mirror.

They had all come to find out where her parents had been. That was crucial. Finding that out told them something. Something that made one of them start the fire.

Her fault.

She remembered the flush of triumph on Isabel's cheeks as she held her. The way she held her even as she squirmed . . . that had been a threat.

Isabel was saying *I can get to your children.*

Amy closed her eyes, remembering the flash of fear and anger on her mother's face. She held on to the sink and leaned over while the words beat inside her. . . .

My fault my fault my fault

Dan banged on the door. "Are you asleep in there?"

Amy opened the door and walked over to the couch. Mechanically, she began to pack.

Nellie shot her concerned glances but Amy always turned away. She couldn't talk about it. If she talked about it, she would crack wide open. She would cry and cry and never stop.

My fault my parents are dead.

Research. That always helped her. If she could get her mind going on a problem, she could forget what she didn't want to remember.

While Shep made pancakes, Amy opened Dan's laptop and searched for anything involving Amelia Earhart and Darwin, Australia. Amy clicked through photographs and found one taken of her at the Darwin airport. She was climbing steps to a building, holding her jacket and a notebook. It could be the very notebook she'd written the letter on! Amy peered closer. Visible on Amelia's pinkie finger was a ring with a white stone. She clicked back to a photograph of Amelia in Bandung. No ring. It must be the ring she'd described, the one the strange man had sold to her.

She tried to magnify the image, but it just became blurry. Dan came over and peered at the screen.

"What are you doing?"

"I'm not sure," Amy admitted. "Do you see the ring on Amelia's finger? It must be the one she bought in Darwin. I'm trying to see it up close. I'm wondering why this guy tried to sell her a ring."

"Well, it sure wasn't a good luck charm," Dan said. He made a noise like a plane spiraling down and crashing. Amy winced.

"It looks like a white stone," she said.

"Probably an opal," Nellie said with a quick look at the computer. She was on her way to the bathroom.

"Most likely," Shep agreed. "Australia has more than ninety percent of the world's opals. Even back then, there was a pretty solid mining trade going on, I'd imagine."

"He said they were in a hole but not to worry," Amy quoted.

Shep grinned. "In a hole? Sounds like Coober Pedy. It means 'white man in a hole' in Aboriginal language."

"Coober who?"

"Name of a town, love," Shep said. "Most of the buildings are underground because it's so freakish hot. Even for Australia. And it's the number one town in the world for mining opals."

"Where is it?" Dan asked.

"Oh, a bit north of Adelaide. About nine hours' drive."

That didn't sound like *a bit,* but maybe it was for

Australia. Amy felt her excitement growing. They were getting close to something, she could feel it. She knew Dan could feel it, too.

"How long did our parents stay in Adelaide?" Dan asked.

"Let's see . . . I picked up some tourists in Perth and flew them to Alice Springs and Uluru . . . or was it Shark Bay and Ningaloo . . . can't remember, but I think I was gone three or four days. Then I swung on down to Adelaide to pick up Hope and Arthur for the Darwin trip."

Amy and Dan exchanged a glance. They didn't have to say it out loud. They knew it. Their parents had gone to Coober Pedy. They'd driven up from Adelaide. They just hadn't wanted to involve Shep more than they had to. It could have put him in danger. Amy and Dan nodded at each other.

Shep pointed the spatula to Amy and then to Dan. "How did you just do that? You two just had a conversation without saying a word!"

They looked at each other again. *It's not that we don't trust him. It's that our parents were right—the less he knows, the better off he is.*

"You just did it again! What are you saying?" Shep put his hands on his hips. "Wait a minute. Hold the phone. You want me to fly you to Coober Pedy, don't you."

Dan smiled innocently. "Your pancakes are burning," he said.

After a breakfast of slightly charred pancakes, they loaded their gear into Shep's Jeep and took off for the airfield. The sun was rising as they left the outskirts of Sydney and took a smaller road, snaking up into the hills. Finally, Shep pulled up to a wire gate and punched in a code. The gate opened and they roared in.

"Congratulations," Shep said. "You just passed through airfield security."

He parked the car and pointed out the plane.

"Um, it looks kind of . . . small?" Amy offered.

"Small? I can fit fourteen in that baby," Shep said.

"You're a good pilot," Nellie said. "Right?"

Shep shrugged. "Except for those crash landings." Chuckling, he headed off to the office.

"Funny cousin you've got there," Nellie said with a yawn.

"C'mon, let's check out the plane," Dan said.

They circled around it, and Nellie climbed inside the cockpit. Dan followed. Amy stood outside, trying to imagine being high above. She'd been in a high-speed helicopter at night and that was terrifying; she'd been swept up by a paraglider, but somehow this small plane made her feel even more nervous. Maybe because she had time to think about how small it seemed and how wide the sky was in Australia.

When Shep headed out of the office and ambled toward them, it only increased her nerves. Shouldn't a pilot be wearing a uniform? It was just Shep, in his khaki shorts and a syrup stain on his T-shirt.

"Are, um, w-we sure about this?" she asked, climbing in.

"Are you kidding?" Dan said, bouncing in his seat.

Nellie was staring out of the cockpit window. She didn't answer.

"Nellie?"

Amy followed her gaze. She saw a plume of dust, rising straight beyond the scrub bushes.

Shep climbed into the plane, instantly making it feel smaller.

"It's a willy willy!" Dan called, pointing at the column of dust.

"A who?" Amy asked.

"A kind of harmless tornado," Shep said, sliding into the pilot seat. "And that isn't one. We don't get willy willys around here. I think it's just a truck going fast on a dirt road. Strap in, everyone. We've got clearance to take off." He put headphones on.

Dan looked disappointed as he strapped into his seat. Nellie buckled in, still peering out at the dust. "It's not a truck," she said. "It's a Hummer. Can we get going?" she asked with sudden impatience in her voice.

"Got to finish the preflight check," Shep said amiably. Just then the speeding Hummer crashed through the metal gate. Shep didn't hear it over the noise of the engine whirring to life.

"Can you hurry?" Amy asked. Shep couldn't hear her, but he gave her a thumbs-up from the cockpit.

Isabel Kabra was at the wheel of the Hummer. She screeched to a halt. Amy saw her head swiveling, squinting through the bright sunlight, trying to see inside the cockpits of the planes.

Slowly, the propeller of Shep's plane started to turn.

"All righty, here we go," Shep said. The plane started to swing toward the runway.

Isabel's head snapped back. She was wearing big black sunglasses, but Amy almost thought she could see the glint of her eyes.

The plane taxied toward the runway.

Amy, Dan, and Nellie watched as Isabel jerked the Hummer with a squeal of tires. To their surprise, Isabel sped off in the opposite direction. But when Shep turned onto the runway, they saw Isabel pull into the field near the runway.

"What's that blasted car doing there?" Shep asked.

"Sightseers?" Nellie suggested.

Shep taxied forward. They picked up speed. Amy relaxed against the seat. Isabel had been foiled. She was probably furious.

"Nyah, nyah," Dan muttered.

As their speed increased, Isabel suddenly cut the wheel and bumped onto the runway.

"What the . . ." Shep exclaimed.

She gunned the motor of the Hummer. Amy could clearly see the terrified faces of Natalie and Ian in the backseat. Natalie had her mouth wide open in a scream.

"I can't stop. I've got to take off!" Shep yelled.

"Go!" Nellie screamed.

The plane lifted, clearing the Hummer by inches.

The last thing Amy saw was Isabel's face. Completely calm. Natalie was still screaming. Isabel was willing to risk her children's lives to stop them.

As soon as they were at cruising altitude, Shep tore off his headphones. "What was that?" he shouted. "That crazy Hummer almost killed us all! Did you see who was driving?"

"Did you see, Amy?" Dan asked.

"The sun was in my eyes," Amy said. "Nellie?"

"That was just too scary," Nellie said.

"I'm going to radio the airport and get that idiot arrested," Shep said. He put his headphones back on and began to speak rapidly into the headset.

Dan and Amy exchanged a glance. There was no way anybody was going to arrest Isabel Kabra. And she was on their tail.

CHAPTER 15

They flew along the coastline, aquamarine water below and stretches of golden sand. Amy's head began to nod, and she fell asleep. No wonder, Dan thought. His sister had tangled with sharks and poison needles, all in one day. That could wear a dude out.

After an hour, even a postcard view couldn't keep his attention. Dan got tired of looking for kangaroos out the window. He hadn't been this bored since Amy forced him to babysit her Barbies when he was five. He started to wonder about the Land Down Under. What was it under, exactly? He almost woke Amy up to ask her but decided it wasn't such a great idea.

Shep's voice came over a speaker. "There are snacks in the cabinet under the sink."

"Dude! You're speaking my language!" But Shep couldn't hear him. Dan got up and foraged.

By the time Amy woke up, they were flying over red ground, vast and empty, and Dan had struck up a beautiful friendship with Australian snack food.

"How long has it been like this?" Amy asked, yawning.

Dan was chewing on a potato chip. "Forever. But check this out." He held up a bag of chips. "These are chicken flavored! Is that genius or what? Are you hungry? I've got Tim Tams, Cheezels, Toobs, and Burger Rings. Can you imagine making a snack that tastes like a *burger*? Australians are our *friends*. And look, Violet Crumbles—the best chocolate bar in the world!"

"Don't spoil your appetite, mate," Nellie called in her Aussie accent. She was now wearing the bush hat Dan had bought in the airport. "We might be stopping for a tick at a chew and spew."

"Chew and spew!" Dan laughed and sprayed potato chips. "Love it!"

"Try the chew part," Amy said. "Lose the spew."

Shep stretched and yawned.

"Want to take a break?" Nellie asked. "I can take over for awhile." At Shep's inquisitive look, she said, "I've been flying since I was a teenager."

"That wasn't so long ago. I'm not reassured."

Nellie grinned. "Trust me. I've got a pilot's license. Five hundred hours. Instrument flying. Night flying."

She and Shep started talking about wind shifts, thrusts, and passenger loads. Dan leaned over to Amy.

"Did you know Nellie could fly a plane?"

Amy shook her head. "I guess it never came up."

"Lots of things don't come up with Nellie. Until they do."

A flicker of doubt passed between them for a moment, but they shoved it aside.

Nellie took over the controls. Shep watched her for awhile, then stepped back into the cabin to talk to them. He leaned against the bulkhead and crossed his arms.

"Okay, something doesn't smell right," he said. "Did you know the person in that Hummer? Because it doesn't seem like a coincidence that it showed up like that."

Dan put on a look of innocence. "No?"

"Is there something you want to tell me? About what you're really doing in Australia?"

"Okay," Dan said. "I guess it's time we told you the truth."

Amy gave him a *no way* look.

"Back in Massachusetts, Amy and I broke into our school one night. No biggie, right? Except that our assistant principal, Mortimer C. Murchinson, is an alien. At night he takes off his *face* and turns into this eleven-foot-tall thing with eight arms . . ."

". . . who plays for the Boston Celtics," Shep said with a sigh. "I get it." His gaze was searching as it rested on them. Then he turned and started back to the cockpit. "If you see any stealth bombers coming our way, just give a yell, okay?"

"You got it, Captain," Dan answered.

Nellie flew the plane for the next hour, then Shep took over for the approach to Coober Pedy.

"Where is it?" Dan asked, craning his neck. All he could see for miles and miles was red dirt. The horizon was curved, as though he could see the edge of the earth.

"See those pyramids?" Shep's voice came over the loudspeaker.

"They look like little hills of salt," Dan said to Amy.

"Those are the slag heaps from opal mining," Shep explained. "We're going to fly right over the opal fields. I reached my mate Jeff this morning. He'll pick us up."

The plane eased down on the runway and rolled to a stop. The airfield was even smaller than the one outside Sydney. There were a few outbuildings and a couple of bush planes. They tumbled out and were hit by a wall of heat. Dan's throat felt as dry as the dusty hills. Shep jumped down, looking as fresh as when he'd begun.

"Is it always this hot?" Dan asked Shep.

"Oh, it's cool today. Only a hundred or so. Let me deal with a bit of paperwork and then I'm guessing Jeff will show up."

Shep ambled into the office, emerging just as a dirt-caked four-wheel-drive truck roared down the road to the airfield. A tall, slim man wearing the usual khaki shorts jumped out.

"They let you land in that shonky orange crate?" he shouted in an Australian accent.

"Next time, I'll land it on your head," Shep answered. "It's big enough."

They clapped each other on the shoulders. Shep turned to them.

"Let me introduce you to my long-lost cousins," he said. "Amy, Dan, and their au pair, Nellie Gomez. This is Jeff Chandler, best tour guide in the Red Centre."

"Mates of Shep's are mates of mine," Jeff said. "What brings you to Coober Pedy? A little noodling?"

"We just had lunch," Amy said politely. She fanned away an enormous black fly. "But thank you."

He laughed. "No, noodling's what we call searching for opals in the slag heaps. Lots of tourists love it. Odds aren't good you'll come up with a valuable stone, but there's always a chance, isn't there?"

"Actually, my rellies are here looking for some information," Shep said. "About someone who might have lived around here in the thirties. He had a scarred face, and back in Sydney he was known as a criminal called Bob Troppo. He didn't speak and he might have been crazy."

"Let's see. Scars on his face, criminal, keeps to himself, mad as a cut snake," Jeff said. "Sounds like half the population of this place." He laughed at Amy's and Dan's crestfallen expressions. "No worries. I know just who to consult. Climb aboard."

They piled in, and he swung out onto the dusty road

and hit the gas hard. He pointed to the opal fields. "If you go out there, you've got to keep your wits about you. Every year we lose a couple of tourists in the open mine shafts. They back up to snap a photo, and *whoosh*, down they go, and come a cropper. Got to tell you, we find it very annoying."

"I bet it annoys the tourists more," Dan said.

"No drama, they're already dead." Jeff drove through the center of town, which wasn't very big. It looked like a Wild West town from a movie. The surrounding area was barren as the moon. The few people on the street wore broad-brimmed hats, and many of the men had long hair and mustaches. From every corner signs shouted OPALS and UNDERGROUND MOTEL. There was even a sign for an underground church.

"Where is everybody?" Nellie asked.

"In the mines or in their homes about now," Jeff said. "Which means underground. Most of us live in dugouts here. They keep us cool during the day and warm at night."

"Wow," Dan said. "This is really the Land Down Under."

"You've got it, mate! Population comes and goes—it's about two thousand right now. And we've got about forty-five different nationalities, everybody looking to strike it rich. We all get along pretty well, until somebody decides to blow something up. Maybe we should stop selling dynamite in the supermarket, eh?"

"He's kidding, right?" Nellie asked Shep.

"Afraid not."

Jeff had slowed on the main drag but picked up speed on the outskirts of town. He roared along the dirt road with all the windows open. At least they'd left the flies behind.

"Here we are!" he called suddenly.

They were in a desolate area. Hills surrounded them, and they could see the now-familiar pyramid shapes of opal mining.

"Which is . . . where?" Nellie asked.

"Kangaroo Ken's place," Jeff said, grinning. "Don't believe a word he says, but he does know everything about Coober Pedy."

With that dubious endorsement, he jumped out of the car and headed toward one of the hills. Now they could see a multicolored door set into the hillside. As they drew closer, they saw that the door was decorated with countless flattened beer cans nailed to its surface.

"Interesting décor," Nellie said.

"You ain't seen nothing yet," Shep said.

"I can get you a mate's rate if you care to spend the night. Ken rents out rooms, too." Jeff opened the door without knocking and shoved his head inside. "Coooeee!" he shouted. "You home? It's Jeff, mate! Got some folks who want to meet you!"

"No need to shout, just come on in before you let in all the blowies, you blooming twit!" a voice roared back.

Jeff winked at them. "Don't let him bother you. He

does the Aussie act for the tourists. He's a bit deaf, so speak up."

They crowded inside and Nellie quickly shut the door. They were in a small hallway. Faint light came from the two small windows near the door. There were hundreds of things tacked to the wall—license plates, bumper stickers in every language, T-shirts, candy wrappers, postcards. The items were so numerous that they were nailed over each other and made a kind of crazy wallpaper. Where there was bare wall, people had scrawled signatures and messages.

"The house was built straight back into the hill, so we're underground right now," Jeff explained as they passed through a kitchen and dining area. The rough walls curved around them. It was like being in a cave, except there was a stove, a refrigerator, a dining table, and a rug on the floor.

They followed Jeff farther into the house, where he led them to a living room lit with lamps. They'd expected to find themselves in some kind of a bunker, but instead they were in a regular room, with a brown couch, a coffee table, a shelf of books, and a TV. It took you a minute to realize the weird part—there were no windows. But after the blasting heat outside, the inside felt cool and comfortable.

An old man sat on the couch, reading a newspaper. He was tanned to the color of a walnut and completely bald. He, too, wore khaki shorts and a T-shirt that read DON'T ASK. He looked over his half glasses at them. "G'day, cobbers. I can see you bunch of galans made it to my shack okay, so pull up a pew and I'll fire up the barbie."

"Stuff the lingo, Kenny," Jeff said. "They're here for a bit of history of Coober Pedy, not your Aussie act."

"You say this is your posse?" the man asked with a chortle. "Knew you'd turn out to be no good." He slapped his knee.

"Aussie act," Jeff shouted. "Oh, never mind. These folks need some information." He raised his voice. "Did you ever hear of a bloke called Bob Troppo?"

"We think he might have lived here in the 1930s," Amy said in a loud voice. "He could have been a miner, but we're not sure about that. We're not sure of his name, but it could have been Bob. His face was scarred on one side and he didn't speak."

"Go on."

"We think he knew someone here . . . someone who sold a ring to Amelia Earhart."

"Blimey," Ken said. "I thought that was just old Ron taking the mick."

"You've heard the story?"

"My own dad told it! Right before the war, he took a trip up to Darwin with some loose opals and some jewelry. He told me the story about how Earhart bought a ring off him. Typical of my dad—he'd tell you some whopping tall tale, and you couldn't prove it didn't happen."

"Well, it did," Dan said. "We know that for sure."

"Too bad he's not around to rub it in." The old man laughed.

"What about the scarred man?" Amy asked.

"Sounds like Fossie," Ken said. "My dad called him that because he got lucky fossicking."

Amy and Dan looked blank.

"Same as noodling," Jeff explained. "Searching for opals on the heaps of sand that get dug out for a mine. It takes some patience, let me tell you."

"Fossie made more money fossicking than mining. He was a strange one. Didn't talk, just stared right past you. A few kangaroos loose in the top paddock, for certain."

"Has anyone else besides us ever asked about him?" Dan asked. He was hoping for news of their parents.

"Eh?"

Dan repeated the question, louder this time. "Not a one," Ken said. "Not many left in Coober Pedy who remember him, and we keep things to ourselves. Besides, Fossie didn't socialize at the pub. He died before Coober Pedy really took off."

Nellie's face changed, and Amy knew she was trying not to smile at the notion that dusty Coober Pedy had taken off. She looked as if she'd just inhaled pepper and was trying not to sneeze.

"Did you ever meet him?" Dan asked.

"Once. He didn't welcome visitors, I'll tell you that. But when he was dying, he called my dad over, and I went with him. I was just a lad then. He left my dad his mine. Nothing much to it, we never did get a stone out of it. After that, he went on a walkabout and never came back. Died out there, alone, just as he wanted."

"Do you know where he lived?"

"Too right I do! Lived right in the mine. Dug a room next to it. Many did in those days. He was the first to figure out a ventilation system, get the whole system working right."

Amy and Dan exchanged a glance. *Ekat.*

"Can we see it?"

"Sure, it's just down the hall."

"Wait a second," Amy said. "Are you telling us that Bob — I mean, Fossie — lived *here*?"

"Well, not *here* here," Ken said, gesturing around the room. "My dad dug out more of the hill and made the house. Fossie just carved out a tunnel and mined straight back into the hill. He dug out a room for himself."

"Is the room still here?" Amy asked.

He nodded. "Sure. We just slapped up a wall to block the mine. But Fossie's room is still there. Shazzer made it up as one of the guest rooms. She was my third wife."

"Your fourth, I think," Jeff said. "And my mum, if you'll recall. You were my stepdad for about two years."

"That's right!" Ken laughed. "How are you, sonny? Sure, have a look," he said to Amy and Dan. "It's been fifty years at least, so I don't think you'll find a thing. But you're welcome to try."

CHAPTER 16

A short while later, Amy sat back on her heels. "Ken's right. There's nothing here. It was all too long ago."

They'd searched the simply furnished room thoroughly, including the small closet. Nothing remained from the home that Bob Troppo had made there.

"I hate dead ends," Dan muttered. "I thought for sure we'd lucked out."

They got up wearily and went back out into the crazily patterned hallway. Amy turned back for a last look and stopped dead. She pointed to the wall on top of the doorway. "Dan, look!"

Amid old postcards from all over the world, crazy drawings, and loopy scrawled messages there was a silly drawing.

"Mom drew this," Amy said breathlessly, pointing to the heart. "I know it. It's drawn with a purple pen! And look, the eyes are red and the smile is blue. She used to make us heart-shaped waffles with strawberries for eyes and a blueberry smile."

"Everybody's mom does that," Dan said.

"But do they do zucchini curls for hair? Look! Green!"

Dan gave her a pained look.

"I liked to dip the zucchini in syrup."

"HA," Dan said.

"Okay, I know it's gross, but—"

"No, HA. It could stand for Hope and Arthur. They *were* here!" Dan shivered with a sudden chill, as though the ghosts of their parents were right there underground with them.

"Do you think they knew we'd come here?" Amy whispered.

Dan shook his head. "They'd never think we'd be going on the clue hunt. Did Grace know about the waffle zucchini thing?"

Amy nodded. "Sure. She made them for me, too."

"It must be a message for Grace, then," Dan said. "They were telling her where to go."

"Where?"

Dan pointed to the last word. "The old mine."

It was late afternoon, but it was still brutally hot. The heat shimmered and bounced. Dan had to squint to see the map that Ken had made for them. They stood on the hill behind Ken's house. Or, Dan corrected in his mind, on *top* of Ken's house.

"It's an old minefield back there, see," Ken had said, "so watch out for mine shafts—they're not all marked. The old ventilation shaft for Fossie's room is still there—you'll see it near the circle of orange flags. Take the first mine shaft past the flags and head down. Then head back the way you came. Easy as pie, not that pie is easy to make, heh!"

They left their bags and Saladin with Ken, who had rooms to rent for the night. Jeff had to get back to work, meeting a busload of tourists, but Shep, Nellie, Amy, and Dan carefully made their way through the field. They saw the orange warning flags, brilliant against the blue sky. "There's the ventilation shaft right there," Shep said, pointing. "So we take the next mine shaft over."

"This isn't exactly what I had in mind when I agreed to bring you here," Shep added, avoiding a mine shaft. "A little sightseeing, a little relaxation, sure. But climbing into an old mine isn't my idea of recreation."

"You don't have to come," Dan said. "You can wait for us at the pub."

"I'm not letting you go down alone," Shep said. "I haven't been there for you in the past, but I can do it now." He grinned. "I'm here to protect you against the ghost of Amelia Earhart. Or the principal without a face."

"Assistant principal," Dan corrected.

"Here we are," Nellie said. She stopped at a shaft. An iron ladder led straight down to a bottom they couldn't see.

"Well, let's get to it," Shep said. "If we don't come up in an hour, Jeff will come looking for us. Unless he forgets."

Shep balanced carefully and started to climb down. Dan went after him. His fingers slipped on the metal, and he gripped it harder, his heart pounding. Why did they always end up underground? Caves, train tunnels, catacombs . . . Were the Cahills vampires? Did they hate the sun?

Nellie swung down, and Amy brought up the rear. It was a long way to the bottom. Darkness crept over them, but there was enough light from the top to barely make out the rungs. Finally, Dan heard Shep's voice. "I'm there. It's about forty feet, I'm guessing." A light switched on.

When his feet finally hit the ground, Dan let out a shaky breath of relief. Not that he'd tell anyone how he felt. But he was creeped out by being so far below, down a little hole.

They had all bought powerful lights in town, and Dan turned his on. The glow illuminated the shaft. A forgotten lantern lay caked with dust in a corner. The walls themselves looked as though they'd been hacked and gouged out by hand.

"All right. If we follow the main tunnel and turn left, we should find Bob's mine," Shep said.

Dan felt his lungs begin to constrict. With every step they disturbed more dust, and he felt the familiar tightness in his chest. "Are you okay?" Amy whispered.

"Fine," he answered. He never liked to admit when he had trouble with his breathing.

Nellie slipped the inhaler into his hand and he took a quick hit. He shot her a grateful look. The tunnel grew narrower. Every few feet they came to another spot that had been worked by a miner. Dan had expected the walls to glitter in many colors like opals, but they were a dull, chalky beige.

The tunnel narrowed further and then twisted sharply right. A pile of rubble lay in front of an opening.

"I think this is it," Shep said. He knelt down and peered over the rubble. Dan looked over his shoulder. Inside the opening was a small cavelike room. The floor was smooth and even. An old stained mattress on an iron bedstead was pushed into a corner. "He must have lived in the mine, as well as that room in Ken's house," Shep said.

Amy and Dan climbed in first. It was a bit brighter in here due to the ventilation shaft that spilled out dim light from a corner.

Amy bent down and picked up a newspaper. She shined her light on it. "It's from Adelaide. The date is 1951. This must be it," she said. "Ken said that Fossie left here in the early fifties. If he was a young man when he assaulted Mark Twain, he must have been close to ninety years old."

Shep stepped inside. "Did you just say assaulted *Mark Twain*?" He held up his hands. "Never mind. Don't tell me."

Dan swept his flashlight over the wall. "Amy, check this out," he said. "He wrote all over the walls." He'd thought it was a design at first, but he realized that it was the words *ring of fire* written in small, cramped handwriting.

The words didn't stop. Tiny, faded in places, in other places covered with dust, the words ran around the entire room, over and over and over, like crazy wallpaper covering every inch of the cavern. Dan and Amy flashed their lights around.

"How long do you think it took?" Amy asked in a hushed voice.

"Years," Shep said, looking around. "You'd have to be pretty crazy to do this," he said with a low whistle.

"Ring of fire," Dan said. "What does that mean?"

"An opal ring?" Amy asked. "They have glints of red and yellow all through them."

Shep went to the far wall and knocked on it. "This isn't solid. This must be the common wall with Ken's house." He stepped closer and accidentally kicked an old toolbox caked with dust. He rapped his knuckles against the wall. "Yeah, this is just drywall. Funny . . ."

"Amy!" Dan shouted. "I found something. A date! It's carved into the rock."

1937 M

"And an M next to it!" Amy exclaimed.

"It might mean that Amelia Earhart *was* a Madrigal," Dan said. "He knew she was looking for him. It was the year the Madrigal came."

"We don't know she was a Madrigal for sure," Amy argued. She couldn't accept that about her childhood hero. "She could have been here trying to *protect* him from Madrigals."

"Our parents must have seen this place," Dan said. "But how did they get in? And out?"

"Maybe Mom and Dad stayed in that room and broke through the wall overnight," Amy said. "Then they repaired it."

"They could have left just a few nails and a hammer out," Shep said, "then pushed the toolbox through the opening. This toolbox doesn't look that old."

"It's not like he would have heard them," Dan said. "Ken can't hear, period."

"Dad was a pretty good carpenter. So was Mom," Amy said. "They did a bunch of renovation work on our old house."

"Hey, maybe we're Ekats!" Dan whispered.

He moved closer to the ventilation shaft and gazed at the wall. "There's a drawing here and some kind of quote."

Partially hidden within the streams of repeating words, they saw:

"That's kind of sad," Amy said.

"Sounds like a Cahill philosophy to me," Dan murmured. "Just tell lies all the time."

"Look at the drawing. It looks like an upside-down ice cream cone. With arrows."

"I prefer sprinkles myself," Dan said.

"I think this is a drawing of this room," Amy said. "I guess this gap here is where the door used to be."

"I hope he didn't quit his day job," Dan said. "He wasn't much of an artist."

"'To be direct and honest is not safe,'" Amy said. "I wonder why he wrote that."

"He didn't," Nellie said. "Shakespeare did. In *Othello*. I played Desdemona in my senior year. We set the play in the future and we all wore aluminum foil costumes. It was a blast."

"Wait a second," Dan said. He got down on his knees and started to search along the wall.

"What are you looking for?" Amy asked.

"It's weird that he wrote the word *safe* right where he did. Maybe he wasn't talking about *being* safe. Maybe he was talking about *a safe.*"

Amy got down on the floor with Dan. They ran their hands along the wall in the corner.

"I found a seam," Amy said excitedly. "We need something for leverage."

Nellie fished in the toolbox and came back with a chisel. Amy slowly worked at the seam. She felt the rock beginning to give. Suddenly, it popped out into her hand.

Dan peered in. "There's an opening carved out."

He stuck his hand in. "I've got something!" His fingers closed around something smooth and cool. He withdrew a small metal box. He opened it. Inside was a leather envelope with a leather cord that wound around it.

Slowly, Dan unwound the cord. He opened the envelope. It was empty. "NOT FAIR!" he yelled.

Amy slumped back in disappointment. "Somebody else got here first!"

"Like our own parents!" Dan tossed the leather envelope aside in frustration.

"Wait." Amy picked up the envelope. She could just make out some faded gold letters on it. "It's a monogram! R C H!"

She looked up at Dan. "Amelia was searching for H, remember? This must be Bob Troppo's real name!"

"But how can we find out who he is?" Dan asked. "We don't know where he was born or where he came from. . . ."

"It's a place to start, anyway." Amy scrambled to her feet. "We need the laptop."

Nellie suddenly put a finger to her lips. "I hear something," she whispered. "Something above . . ."

Dan moved closer to the ventilation shaft. He stood underneath it and looked up. He could hear the sound of voices, but he couldn't see anyone, just a faint circle of blue sky. "This is it," someone said. He saw a shadow and quickly jumped back.

"Eww," someone said, a high-pitched whine. "Don't put them near me."

"That sounds like Natalie Kabra," he whispered.

"I am surrounded by fools," a woman's voice said impatiently. "Hand me the jar."

"That's Isabel," Amy whispered.

Suddenly, something fell through the ventilation shaft. It was black and the size of a salad plate. Dan felt it brush his arm. He looked down and saw the biggest, hairiest spider he'd ever seen. It started to crawl up his arm toward his face. He screamed and backed up to the wall. He was too paralyzed to touch it.

Shep sprang over. "It's all right," he said. He brushed off the spider and it scurried away on the floor. "It's not poisonous."

"I-I think we should move away from the shaft," Amy said.

They all looked at her for a second. Then they quickly sprang back as a shower of spiders began dropping down onto the floor. Soon there was a carpet of scurrying, hairy arachnids waving thick spider legs. Amy screamed.

"Get back!" Shep ordered. He swallowed and pointed to a hairy spider on the ground. "That's a funnel-web. And there's another one . . ."

Dan gulped. He was still shaking from his encounter with the plate-sized spider. "The most venomous spider in the world?"

"It's all right, it's not aggressive," Shep said. "Just . . . don't . . . alarm it."

"H-how do you alarm a spider?" Amy squeaked.

"Should we reason with it?" Nellie asked shakily.

"Okay, here's the good news." Shep scanned the floor rapidly. "I think I only see two."

"You *think*?" Nellie asked, leaping away from one hairy specimen.

The funnel-web spider had scurried in front of the exit. It sat there for a moment, raising its hairy legs and tentatively exploring its new surroundings. The other funnel-web walked along the wall, and they backed away from it.

"Okay," Shep said, scanning the spiders as he kept his eyes on the funnel-webs. "Looks like there are only two funnel-webs, but there are a few red-backs. Not deadly, but they can give a nasty bite. We're going to have to get out of here. But no worries. We'll just—"

With a soft thump, another creature landed in the dust. The snake curled around and raised its head.

They heard Isabel's laugh come down through the shaft. "Yoo-hoo!" she said. "Thought you might be lonesome down there. We sent you some pets!"

Dan swallowed. "Please don't tell me that's what I think it is. . . ."

"Taipan," Shep breathed. "The most . . ."

". . . poisonous snake in the world," Dan finished.

CHAPTER 17

The snake slithered across the small room. Dan didn't think it looked happy about falling forty feet onto the floor.

"Don't panic. Just let it go about its business," Shep said in a whisper.

"I wouldn't dream of interfering," Nellie said, backing away.

"In its venom is a neurotoxin that can cause paralysis," Dan said. "But it also contains a myotoxin. Which means it can break down your muscle tissue . . ."

"We really don't need the details," Nellie said. "Can't we condense it to — don't let it bite ya?"

The orange-brown snake made its way slowly toward the exit to the main tunnel. Its tongue flicked out and in. It must have been seven feet long. They held their breath as its head rose. But it just curled up and rested on the mine floor. They'd have to step over it in order to get out.

Shep reached out and picked up a hammer. "It'll move eventually. We can wait."

Dan felt the familiar squeezing in his chest. His breath came out in a wheeze. He coughed, and Amy shot him a concerned look. "You okay?"

"Okay." He could barely get the word out.

"Dan! Your inhaler!" Nellie's voice was urgent. "It's in your pocket."

He reached into his pocket. Stuffed in there was the packaging from a candy bar, a cool rock he'd found in Shep's garden, and a chunk of granola bar he was saving for later. He tugged, and the inhaler popped out, flew in the air, and landed on the mine floor. It rolled toward the snake.

Everyone's heart seemed to stop. The only sound was Dan's labored breath.

The inhaler stopped rolling just inches from the taipan.

Dan's wheezing got worse, and his hands flew to his chest.

"I'll get it," Nellie said.

"No." Shep's voice was quiet but rang with authority, and he was already moving. He kept the hammer cocked into position in case the snake struck. Shep walked closer. The snake's tongue flickered. Swiftly, Shep kicked the inhaler back toward Nellie. Then he jumped back as the snake moved. It slithered another inch or two, then stopped. Amy let out a shaky breath.

Nellie knocked a spider off the inhaler with her shoe. Quickly, she handed it to Dan.

He felt his lungs open. The rattling breathing eased. But his chest still felt tight. He still struggled. This was a bad one. There was so much dust in the air, and it wasn't helping his nerves to be in a cave full of poisonous creatures. He leaned over as black spots swarmed in his vision. *Panic makes it worse,* he told himself.

"Just keep breathing, nice and slow, Dan-o," Nellie said. She turned to Shep.

"We've got to get Dan out of here. He needs medical attention."

Dan was scared that he didn't have the breath to say *I'm okay.*

A spider crawled up Amy's sneaker, and she yelped and jumped away.

"It's all right, it's not poisonous," Shep told her. He called over to Nellie. "Get the toolbox. Careful, make sure there's nothing crawling in there."

Gingerly, Nellie picked up the toolbox. She handed it to Shep.

"Let's pay Ken a surprise visit," Shep said. "We just have to make a new door. Hang in there, Dan." He swung at the wall with the hammer. A chunk fell off onto the floor.

"Hand me a hammer," Nellie said. "I'll help."

"You two, keep your eyes on the taipan and the spiders," Shep said. "If they move this way, tell me."

He bashed on the wall and it splintered into chunks. Nellie swung with powerful strokes. Within a few minutes, they had cleared a hole in the wall big enough to step through. Dan went first, and then one by one, they climbed into Ken's closet.

Dan sat on the floor, struggling to breathe.

"He needs a doctor," Nellie said anxiously.

"Call Jeff and tell him it's an emergency," Shep said. "And then tell him to call the police."

By the time they reached the doctor, Dan was already feeling better. He was given a checkup and a warning to stay out of the opal mines. Dan agreed immediately.

"That's the first time I've ever heard you say 'yes, sir' to an authority figure and mean it," Nellie said with a grin as they got back into Ken's car. She slung an arm around his shoulders and even kissed the top of his head, but Dan didn't mind. "Don't scare me like that again, dude," she said. "Or else."

"Yeah," Amy added. "Maybe we should leave mines off our itinerary for awhile." She said the words lightly, but she still felt shaky from seeing her brother look so pale and sick.

Ken wasn't happy when he took a peek in his spare room and found out he'd lost a wall in the closet. Not to mention that a number of deadly creatures lay on the other side. With the help of some experts in Coober Pedy, the snake and the spiders were trapped and taken away. The police asked questions, but Dan and Amy had no answers. Shep couldn't seem to lose his worried frown. Finally, Jeff and Shep volunteered to take Ken down to the pub in order to calm him down.

It had been one long day. But Amy was itching to research the initials they'd found on the leather envelope. After a quick dinner, she fired up Dan's laptop.

"Okay," she said, her fingers poised over the keys. "What do we search for? Plugging in the letters RCH is going to get us exactly nowhere."

"I think we should figure that the C maybe stands for Cahill?" Dan suggested.

Amy nodded. "I was thinking the same thing. And if we can place him in Sydney in 1896, let's say he was at least in his twenties? So that means he was born somewhere around . . ."

"The 1870s," Dan said.

Amy opened a search engine. "Okay. Let's start with Robert Cahill something . . . just in case Bob was his real name. I'll try . . . Robert Cahill with Sydney and 1890." Amy groaned as a long list of hits popped up. "Nothing looks promising," she murmured.

"Try 'Darwin,'" Dan suggested. "It's a smaller city."

"Especially back then," Amy agreed.

Amy plugged in "Robert Cahill," "1890s," and "Darwin." Another stream of information came up. She read down the list. "This isn't working, I'm getting all these references to Charles Darwin . . . wait a second . . ." Suddenly, Amy sat up straight. "This has got to be it! I have his name! It's—"

CHAPTER 18

"Robert Cahill Henderson," Isabel repeated into the cell phone. "Got it."

She turned around to talk to the others in the backseat. They'd left Coober Pedy at high speed, but she'd pulled off the road in order to take the call she'd been waiting for.

"It's about time somebody did something right. The Lucian stronghold used their mother computer to analyze all known Ekaterinas from 1840 to 1900. The computer had a match for Coober Pedy and Cahill. Apparently, even mute crazy fools have to use their real name on a mining claim. Robert Cahill Henderson is our man."

"So where do we go next?" Natalie asked, flipping her long silky hair over her shoulder. "I hope it's someplace with good shopping. Dubai?" she asked hopefully.

"Jakarta," her mother said.

"Where is that?" Natalie said, crashing back against the seat. "It doesn't sound glamorous."

"Why am I paying for your education?" Isabel asked. "Jakarta is on Java. Henderson took passage from there on a ship called the *Lady Anne* to Sydney in 1883." Isabel eyed Irina. "What's your problemski, comrade? Are you worried about little Dan and Amy? They seem to have nine lives. They survived. A little scare will keep them on their toes."

Irina said nothing. At her feet was the empty jar and box that the Fixer had delivered to Isabel. Isabel had whistled as she'd carried it herself to the private plane she'd hired to take them to Coober Pedy. She'd also arranged for a Hummer to be driven up from Adelaide.

Irina hadn't known what was in the box until Isabel had opened it. Isabel had smiled as she shook out the jar of deadly spiders. She'd planned on releasing them into the Cahills' hotel room, but this was better still. Right down the shaft onto their heads! Isabel had also handled the snake easily. Not a drop of perspiration on her brow as she flipped the latch and grabbed him from behind, wearing the heavy gloves. She had *enjoyed* it. Enjoyed being close to so much deadly terror.

"I want you to keep track of the Cahill brats while I take Ian and Natalie with me. Report in on their movements. If by some slim chance they're on their way to Java, delay them. I'm tired of them in my hair."

"And then?" Irina asked.

"And then *what*?" Isabel asked irritably. She was

checking her lipstick in the rearview mirror, and she tilted it to look at Irina.

"They aren't going away for long," Irina said. "We have seen their tenacity. What are your ultimate plans for them?"

Isabel shrugged. "I haven't thought that far ahead. I'm concentrating on this clue. We could even find all thirty-nine clues—can you imagine that, children?—because we're almost one hundred percent sure that Robert Cahill Henderson had most, if not all, of them. Amy and Dan will be immaterial. They'll be *dust*. Not worth dealing with." Isabel played with the gold charms on her bracelet, then turned her attention to her fingernails.

Irina watched Isabel's careless indifference, as though her manicure was the most important thing in the world. She knew Isabel too well and for too long. It was true she cared deeply about nail polish. But she also cared deeply about getting rid of dust.

Isabel had used some of her best tricks to scare them away. Soon she would unleash her rage. Irina could feel it building.

This has been a long road, she thought. *Now, I can finally see the end.*

CHAPTER 19

"Robert Cahill Henderson was a brilliant chemist," Amy said, reading rapidly. "He was also engaged to a cousin of Queen Victoria. He was a champion of Darwin's theories. That's why the search engine came up with so many hits. This is fascinating. . . ."

"Yeah. Wake me up when it's over," Dan said. He lay stretched out on one of the twin beds in Ken's spare room. He glanced over at the closet. "Are we sure they caught the snake?"

"We're sure. Anyway, one day he suddenly broke his engagement — which was a huge deal in those days — and took off for the South Seas. He said he was going to do further study on Darwin's theories. But he wasn't a naturalist, he was a chemist," Amy added thoughtfully. "So that's strange."

"Whatevs," Dan said with a yawn. "When does the fascinating part come?"

"He made his way around the islands of Indonesia until settling on one to conduct experiments. He was believed to have perished in the eruption of Krakatau in 1883."

"Krak-a-wa?"

"Krakatau," Amy said. "It was a huge volcanic explosion. Actually, a series of explosions. The mountain basically imploded, and then came these huge tsunamis that killed about thirty-six thousand people. They heard the noise of the final explosion all the way in Australia. The dust cloud that came afterward gave spectacular sunsets even in the United States."

"Now you're getting to the cool part."

"That's it! The upside-down ice cream cone!" Amy said excitedly. "It was a volcano! He was drawing Krakatau. But why did he suddenly leave his fiancée and go to Indonesia? There has to be a reason."

"Sure," Dan said. "He was one smart dude. Get married or go lie on a beach. No contest. Even with the volcano, the dude was ahead."

"So he must have been in the vicinity of Krakatau when it blew. He barely escaped with his life," Amy said. "He got to Sydney somehow. And Cahills and Madrigals have been looking for him ever since. Why?"

If you found something, it belongs to all of us. If you keep it, you are thieves. Simple as that.

It was the strangest thing. Dan's face was in front of her, but she had been gone, for just a moment. Standing in her nightgown, listening to the grown-ups.

"Earth to Amy," Dan said.

She didn't fall asleep until the people left. She heard the front door shut. She looked out to make sure they were really gone. But they stood in a little knot right under her window. She raised it slightly so she could look at them again. All she could see was the top of their heads.

"Get some nerve," the beautiful lady said. "We have our answer. They traced him to Australia. This has to be taken care of tonight."

Her fault.

Her fault.

"Amy? You're wigging." Dan peered at her. "Seriously, are you okay?"

She looked at her brother. At his pale face, the way he was worried about her but trying not to be. The asthma attack had taken so much out of him, but he was pretending it hadn't. She could see the exhaustion in the dark circles under his eyes.

"I'm fine," she said.

"So, what's next, space shot?" Dan asked. "Back to Sydney?"

She cleared her throat. Her voice sounded rusty to her ears. "Darwin. We have to keep following their footsteps."

On the plane the next morning, Amy settled back into the seat and opened the biography of Amelia Earhart she'd borrowed from Shep. She didn't know what she was looking for, so she leafed through the book, reading various passages, while Nellie zoned out with her earbuds and Dan made his way through a package of chicken-flavored potato crisps. A good night's sleep had restored him to his usual ravenous self.

"Dan, listen to this," she called. "In 1935, when Amelia was in Hawaii, she consulted with a noted volcanologist!"

"Fascinating!" Dan said, ripping open a Violet Crumble.

"Don't you see? She could have been gathering information about Krakatau, even then," Amy said.

Dan closed his eyes and gave a huge pretend snore. Amy sighed and took out the pages she'd down-loaded from the Internet and printed out on Ken's printer. She read through accounts of the original explosion. Occasionally, she'd read out an interesting fact to Dan, even though he had taken all his wrappers, balled them up, and was pretending to shoot baskets with them. Then she read a story that made her sit up. She read it slowly again. "Dan!"

"*Swish!* Another three-pointer!"

Amy threw a pillow at him. "DAN! Listen to this. During the day of the eruption, a ship heading for Batavia—that was the name for Jakarta then—got into trouble. They ran into this huge cloud of ash, and then all this pumice—volcanic rock—started to rain on the deck. So the captain pulled into a harbor miles away. They never made it to port, they had to turn around. But get this—the cargo was wolfram."

Dan sat up straight. "Wolfram? That's tungsten, one of the clues."

"Not only that, the captain mentions that they had all these myrrh plants on deck. And the pumice and ash was raining down, so he had to order the crew to take it all below. What are the odds of a ship carrying both tungsten and myrrh?"

"They were bringing clues. Probably to Henderson, right?"

"It *must* have been! He was assembling clues!" Amy cried. "That's it! He was a scientist, so he was working on some kind of formula. Maybe that's why trying to find him is so crucial—why all the branches are looking. He set up some sort of lab. . . ." Amy smacked her chair. "On Krakatau! That's it! He had to order stuff to be delivered. And then when Krakatau blew . . . the lab was destroyed. He must have gotten caught in the tsunami . . . but he survived."

"So the only thing left . . . was in his head," Dan said. "And he was nuts."

Amy nodded, remembering the crazy obsessive writing in the mine. "I bet we're right that he was an Ekat. He attacked Mark Twain, so he can't be a Janus. And Isabel doesn't seem to know much about him, so he can't be a Lucian. He sure didn't *look* like a Tomas."

Dan frowned. "We know that a Lucian—Constantine of Russia—had found most of the clues early in the nineteenth century. It seems like two of the branches were getting pretty close back then."

Amy tapped the papers. "You know what else is in here? The island of Java is part of this whole area of volcanoes in the Pacific called the Ring of Fire. RCH wasn't talking about opals. He was talking about Java. That's where we have to go next!"

Nellie took over the piloting and Shep came back to stretch out in one of the seats. He blinked when Amy and Dan mentioned Jakarta.

"I said I'd do anything for you, and I will, but my plane doesn't have the range," he said. "I'd guess it's about sixteen or seventeen hundred miles. You'll be better with a commercial flight. Plenty of those from Darwin. I've got a satellite phone—I can set you up right from here." Shep hesitated. "I trust Nellie to take care of you. But is there any chance you can pass on Java? Danger seems to be tailing you guys—that, or some incredible bad luck. You could hang out with me for awhile. Not that I'm a father figure or anything . . . just a surfing bum. Can't you not do . . . whatever it is that you won't tell me you're doing?"

Amy blinked back sudden tears. "We'd be honored to hang with a surfing bum like you." She swallowed hard. "But we have to do this."

Shep held her gaze for a minute. Then he nodded. "I never tried to talk Artie out of anything, either."

While Shep made arrangements, Amy looked down. They were flying over red earth and tall cliffs, a dark blue river snaking through a canyon. It was spectacularly beautiful.

"Katherine Gorge," Shep told her, hanging up. "There are some amazing sights here in the Top End."

"I wish . . ." Amy said. She didn't complete the thought. *The next time I go around the world, it would be nice to actually see it.*

"I've got you on a flight leaving about an hour after we arrive," Shep said. "It's going to be tight, but I know the airport. We can swing it." He looked at Amy and Dan. "Things will be hectic when we get there, so it seems like a good time to tell you that if you ever need anything from me, it's yours. I won't fail you guys again."

"Thanks," Amy said. "And you didn't fail us."

"You helped us when someone else would have screamed and run," Dan said. "Cousins for life."

"And one more thing," Shep said. "So far I've been chased off my favorite beach, almost crashed into on a runway, almost killed in a mine, and had to entertain the biggest bore in Coober Pedy in a pub for two hours. Not to mention that I've grown fond of you three. So out with it. The truth. I think I deserve to know. What's really going on? And leave out the aliens."

Amy and Dan looked at each other.

"Okay," Amy said, blowing out a breath. "Our grandmother Grace left a will that gave us a choice between a million dollars and a hunt to find thirty-nine clues, which, when we put them together, will make us the most powerful people in the world. So we chose the hunt. Along with various assorted horrible Cahill relatives, all of whom have tried to kill us at one time or another."

Shep sighed. "If you don't want to tell me, I guess that's up to you."

Within an hour, the city of Darwin loomed ahead, curling around a beautiful harbor. Beyond lay a vast blue sea. They landed and ran through the airport to Qantas Airlines.

"This is impossible," they heard a voice say. "There *have* to be seats in first class."

The desk clerk leaned over to murmur. Amy, Dan, and Nellie backed up behind a pillar. Shep followed curiously. "What's up, gang? Another pack of blood-thirsty aliens?"

"You got it," Dan said.

"We can't get on that plane," Amy whispered.

Shep peered around the pillar at Isabel, Natalie, and Ian. "They don't look so bad to me."

"They just tried to kill you with the most venomous snake on the planet," Dan said.

"We've *got* to get to Java," Amy said.

Shep shook his head. "This is just too dangerous. I can't let you go."

Amy gave him a level look. There was no pleading in it, only determination.

"You said you'd be there for us, no matter what."

Reluctantly, Shep nodded. "I don't like it, but okay. Time for Plan B. Let's check out the pilots' lounge."

Shep took them to the part of the airport where chartered flights came in. He walked into the plush lounge as though he owned it and scanned the room.

"We are in luck," he whispered to Amy, Dan, and Nellie. "I see somebody who owes me a favor."

They followed in his wake as he moved casually toward a tall man in a pilot's uniform who was sitting with a cup of coffee by the window.

"Greg!" Shep called. "Fancy seeing you here, mate!"

"Shep, haven't seen you in donkey's years. When are you going to get respectable and find a real job?"

"Never, I guess." Shep quickly introduced them. "Thing is, mate, we're in a bit of a jam. We need to get to Jakarta. And I happen to remember that you owe me a favor."

"No, mate. You owe *me* a favor."

"What? Remember that turn I did for you back in Brissie last year?"

"Paid you back in Perth last December."

Shep scratched his head. "So you did. Well, have you got a job going right now?"

"Just got back from one. Taking a few weeks off."

"Perfect! Then I'm about to owe you another favor." Shep grinned at his friend. "Loan me your plane."

They didn't know how he arranged it, but he did. As part of a charter service, they were whisked through security. They waited in the cushy lounge while Shep handled the details of departure.

"All right," Shep said, rubbing his hands together. "We're all set. Hangar Eight. I can't wait to get my hands on this plane. It's a luxury prop jet. Awesomely sweet."

"You really came through for us," Amy said. "Thanks."

"I'm doing this for Artie and Hope," Shep answered. "And you two. We're family. I think after all these years, I finally get what that means. So I owe you a bigger thanks."

"Family, dude." Dan held out a fist, and Shep did the same. They bumped knuckles.

"Family," Amy repeated. She bumped knuckles with Shep, too.

Shep cleared his throat. "All right. Now let's get on the plane before I change my mind."

They were met with a blast of humid air as they exited the lounge and walked to the plane. Dan climbed the steps and peeked inside. It was luxurious, with plush seats, a dining area, and screens at every seat. "Whoa," Dan said. "Traveling in style! At last!"

"We've got about an eight-hour flight," Shep said. "There should be plenty of food stocked aboard, and movies, games, whatever you want." He turned to Nellie. "Bet you haven't seen one of these babies before."

"Actually, I've flown one from Akron to Reykjavik," Nellie said.

"Whoa, Madame Mysterioso," Shep said. "What kind of au pair are you?"

"I just like to fly," Nellie said.

"I can see my cousins are in good hands," Shep said to her. "Cool in the face of a taipan snake and capable of flying a plane overseas. Awesome combo."

Amy frowned at Dan. Just how many more surprises was Nellie going to pull?

Just then several uniformed officers came toward them. "Excuse me, sir," the tallest one said politely to Shep. "May I see your passport?" The officer held out his hand.

"We've already gone through security," Shep said.

"Your passport, please." The officer's voice was firm.

Shep checked the pockets of his shorts. "I thought I had it here. Hang on."

"Can you all come with us, please?"

"It's them! It's my babies!" The voice echoed across the hangar.

A woman in a black dress hurried into the hangar, clasping her hands together. It took them a moment to recognize Irina. She was wearing a scarf tied under her chin and small rimless glasses.

"There they are, my little pierogies!" she cried. "Are you all right? Did he hurt you?"

"Did who hurt us?" Dan asked.

"This woman claims to be your cousin," the officer said.

"She is," Amy admitted, "technically, but . . ."

The officer turned to Shep. "In that case, you're under arrest for kidnapping."

CHAPTER 20

"This is ridiculous!" Shep said as they walked back into the hanger. "I'm their cousin, too!"

"You see how he makes big lie from mouth," Irina said, pressing her handkerchief to her eyes. Her Russian accent had thickened. *"Maya morkovka!"* she cried to Amy. "My little carrot! How my eyes have longed to plant themselves on your face!"

Amy grabbed Shep's arm. "He *is* our cousin!"

"May I see your passport, sir?" the officer asked Shep sternly.

"I just had it a minute ago. . . ."

"Come here, little treasure," Irina said, trying to hug Dan. "I am like grandmother to these children. They ran away from guardian in Boston. You see I have papers. Look! Office Social Services, city of Massachusetts, have been looking. I have been sent to bring them home."

"Everything looks in order," the officer said, consulting the papers. "Apparently, Social Services are looking for these two back in the States."

"That woman is a lying, homicidal spy!" Dan cried, pointing at Irina.

"She tried to kill us!" Amy yelled.

Irina dabbed at her eyes again, which were completely dry. "They have always had trouble with authority," she said to the officer. "You know American children, so spoiled. But they are my little pierogies, and I love them. They are family."

"You say you're their nanny *and* their cousin?" the officer asked.

"Oooooo," Irina cried, throwing her handkerchief over her face. "My heart in broken pieces like teacup, just seeing sweet angel faces again!"

"My heart is throwing up in mouth," Nellie said, rolling her eyes.

Even the security officer lifted an eyebrow. Amy thought Irina was piling it on a little too thick. Obviously, she didn't have much practice at sentiment.

"If you could let me go back to the plane, I could get the papers," Shep said. "I've clearly misplaced them, but they can't have gone far."

"Don't move." The officer turned to Amy and Dan. "This lady is Irina Cahill, and she claims—"

"She's not a Cahill!" Amy cried. "I mean, she is, but that's not her name!"

The officer wiped some sweat from his forehead. "Can everybody stop shouting? We're trying to straighten this out."

Another officer hurried from the building. He whispered in the head officer's ear. Amy heard the word *Interpol*.

The head officer turned to Irina. "Do you happen to know an Irina Spasky?"

"Never heard of this person." Irina looked blank. "Spasky is common Russian name."

"*She's* Irina Spasky!" Amy yelled.

"This person is wanted by Interpol for . . . uh, various international crimes." The officer consulted the list. "Dubrovnik, 2002, traveling under false passport. Sofia, 1999, administering paralyzing poison to unidentified male. Sri Lanka . . ." The officer looked pale. "Crikey."

"That's her!" Dan cried. "Lock her up and throw away Russian key!"

Irina smiled. "Silly children. Tell me, officers, why aren't you chasing criminals like this Spasky, not accusing poor Russian nanny trying to save children from kidnapper."

The officer sighed. "So you say, ma'am."

Shep began to talk to the officer, explaining that he was Arthur Trent's cousin and a respectable citizen with a flight plan and a plane he needed to take off in. He pulled Nellie into the discussion.

Irina turned to Amy and Dan. She lowered her voice to a whisper.

"I am here to help you. You are flying straight into a trap."

"Hello? It seems to me that we're already in one," Dan said.

"Can't resist chance to needle me," Irina said. "I understand."

"You're the one with the needles," Dan pointed out.

"We're not going to get caught in your trap," Amy said fiercely. "You probably thought you killed us back in that mine—"

"I was not involved in what happened," Irina said. "I didn't know what Isabel was planning until she did it. I would have stopped her if I could."

"Liar!"

"Haven't you figured out who your real enemy is yet?"

Dan pointed to Irina. "Bingo!"

"Don't go to Jakarta. If Isabel knows you're there, she will kill you, do you understand?"

"And suddenly you're some sort of grandma?" Dan asked scornfully. "Please. You would have killed us if you had the chance."

"Amy." Irina said her name quietly. Amy had never heard that tone in Irina's voice. She couldn't quite figure it out at first, but then she got it. The *scorn* was missing.

"Isabel told you it was me who killed your parents. Correct?"

Amy only stared at her.

Dan's head whipped from Irina to Amy and back again. "What did she just say?"

"She lied. She will lie about anything to get what she wants. Have you remembered more about that night?"

"Our parents were murdered?" Dan asked in a whisper. He turned his bewildered gaze on Amy. He looked like a lost little boy. It was exactly the look she had dreaded seeing.

"Yes," Amy said. "I remember you." She made the accusation coolly, hoping Irina would take the bait. Irina must have been there, even if she couldn't remember her.

"But not just me, correct?"

"What is going on?" Dan's voice wavered.

"Why?" Amy asked. She forced the words out around the tightness in her throat. "How could you do it?"

"I didn't," Irina said. "Yet, I was there."

"That's called accessory to murder," Amy said.

Dan's face had seemed to shrink in his bewilderment. He looked as though somebody had kicked him hard in the stomach.

Shep's voice grew louder. "If you'd just let me back on my plane!"

"Not your plane, I think," the officer said. "It is leased from a Mr. Gregory Tolliver, and we're trying to contact him. Unfortunately, his mobile is off."

"He's a mate of mine," Shep said. "He'll vouch for me."

"Well, if I can't reach him, he can hardly do that."

"I'm just saying—"

"Accessory, no," Irina said rapidly to Amy. "I walked away. But at least one of us remained. Do you remember who?"

"Why don't you tell me?"

"Because *you* must remember."

"You keep hinting that it's Isabel. I know what you want me to say. So what's the difference between the two of you? She accuses you, and you accuse her."

Irina's face drained of color. "What is the difference between us," she repeated. "I'm finding that out."

"Can we go back to the lounge, please?" Nellie asked the officer. "This is very upsetting for the children."

Irina's hand gripped Amy's wrist. "You must believe me —"

"Hey! Hands off my cousin!" Shep ordered. "Are you going to let her do that?" he said to the officer. For a split second, he looked at Amy. He raised his fist and punched the air lightly. *Family,* Amy thought. It was like Shep was saying good-bye.

Irina dropped Amy's hand, but she leaned in closer. "I cannot stop you," she said rapidly. "But remember my warning. That's the best I can hope for now."

"All right," the officer said to Nellie, distracted as Shep began arguing with Irina. "But don't leave the lounge!"

"Too right! She'll be apples!" Nellie said cheerfully, and pulled Dan and Amy away. As soon as they were out of earshot, she murmured, "Back to the plane."

"What?" Amy asked.

"Shep slipped me the documentation. It was in his shorts. We're good to go."

"Can you fly that thing?" Amy asked nervously.

"Cake," Nellie said.

"But what about the security guys?" Dan asked.

"That's why we have to do it fast," Nellie said. "And casually."

"How do you steal a plane casually?" Dan asked.

"Like this."

Nellie strolled over to the plane. She gave a quick look back, then ran up the stairs. Amy and Dan followed.

"Buckle up. I'll radio the tower. Shep told me there was a good chance they hadn't rescinded the flight information yet. By the way . . ." Nellie turned around briefly to grin at them, "he said good luck."

Amy and Dan buckled in nervously as Nellie spoke to the control tower. The plane rolled out onto the runway. Amy pressed her nose against the window. Shep was waving his arms and talking to the security officers, who were completely unaware that the plane was taxiing away.

Irina stood unmoving, her gaze on the plane. At any moment, Amy expected her to alert the officers. But she just stood and watched.

Why was she just letting them go?

"We're off!" Nellie called as the plane picked up speed. Soon they were barreling down the runway. Amy gripped the armrest. She sure hoped Nellie hadn't exaggerated her piloting skills.

"Do you think we have parachutes?" she asked Dan. He didn't answer. He, too, was gripping the armrest.

The plane lifted off smoothly. It rose in the air, banked over the city of Darwin, and headed out across the green water.

Nellie's voice came over the PA system. "Okay, passenger peeps, just sit back and enjoy the ride. Next stop, Java."

Amy leaned closer to Dan. "It's so weird, all these things we're finding out about Nellie," she said. "It's like she's been *trained* for this." Dan didn't answer. He was staring out the window, his face tight and strained. "I'm beginning to wonder if we really know her at all."

Dan turned on her fiercely. "I know how that feels."

"What?" Amy asked.

"Isabel told you that Irina killed our parents? And you didn't tell me?"

Amy could see the tips of Dan's ears glowing red, the way his mouth twisted. His eyes filled with tears.

"I was going to tell you, it's just that . . ."

It's just that I keep getting these flashes. And sometimes I don't know if they're real. And I'm scared, Dan. Really scared. What if it's my fault they died?

"Oh, and when was that going to be?" Dan's mouth set in a line. "Tomorrow? Next week? Or never?"

"It seemed like it was better to wait." Even to Amy's ears, her explanation sounded lame.

"Our parents were *murdered,* and you found out who did it, and you didn't tell me?"

"We don't know it was Irina!"

"And you *believe* her?"

"Well, it's not like we can trust Isabel. She tried to feed me to the sharks, remember? And she tried to kill us in the mine. Hello? She doesn't sound like the most trustworthy person, either."

"I deserve to know. You're treating me like . . . like a baby brother!"

"You *are* my baby brother!"

"I'm not a baby!" Dan's face was like a fist, screwed up tight. "I saved your sorry butt enough times. You counted on me enough times to get you out of places when you were too scared to move. So why do you think you have to protect me?"

Because you're my baby brother, Amy wanted to say.

But she couldn't say it. She knew if she did, Dan just might jump out of the plane, with or without a parachute.

So she just looked at him, helpless.

"Secrets and lies," he said. "Congratulations, sister. You've officially turned into a Cahill."

CHAPTER 21

If there was one thing Dan never expected to hear in his life, it was *Next stop, Java* as his au pair took off across a sea that stretched in every direction.

If there was one thing he never thought he'd feel, it was this alone.

Once, when he was seven, he'd run into a sliding glass door. Straight into it, and flat-out running. He'd bounced back and landed on the ground. He still remembered that feeling of sudden, violent shock. And right after that, the pain.

Now he felt exactly the same way.

His parents dying was something he tried not to think about, but of course he thought about it almost every day. He especially tried not to think about goopy stuff like *what if*. What if Dad was around to take him to soccer? What if Mom had been there for his worst asthma attack? He told himself that it was babyish to have those thoughts. The fire happened. It was fate. Nothing he could change about it. Nobody to blame.

Except there *was* somebody to blame. Someone had

stolen his family. Someone had stolen his childhood. Someone had, one chilly night, deliberately gone into a house with four people *who loved each other* and set a fire.`. . .

Dan shook his head violently. He felt his legs trembling. He looked out at the vast sea. Aunt Beatrice used to say, *Aren't our problems so small when we look at something big, like the sky?* That was her way of comforting two kids whose parents had died. Aunt Beatrice was an idiot.

The Indian Ocean didn't make him feel one bit better. It would be easier if he could talk to Amy, but he'd pretty much decided he'd never talk to her again.

He'd been angry at Amy lots of times. *Way* lots. This was worse than when she'd made tiny little dolls for all his Matchbox cars right before his best friend, Liam, came over. Worse than when she told Aunt Beatrice that he loved Beethoven so she should sign him up for piano lessons. Worse than back in Egypt, when he thought she was grabbing all of their memories of Grace for herself.

That was nothing compared to this.

She'd found out his parents had been murdered, and she'd kept it secret. The most important thing in their lives!

The fire hadn't been accidental. It hadn't been because his father hadn't banked the fire and a spark had hit the rug. Someone had gone in and deliberately set it.

And Amy had known. She'd even been downstairs that night! And she'd never told him.

He'd thought they were together. In everything.

He stared out at the green water stretching to the horizon. He didn't know how to get over this. He didn't know how to deal with it. His parents. Grace. Now Amy.

There was nobody left.

It was still light as Nellie landed the plane expertly at Halim Perdanakusuma International Airport, south of the city of Jakarta. She took off her earphones and let out a breath. "I'm totally beat," she said.

She slung her bag over her arm and picked up Saladin's carrier. "If we run into trouble at customs, let me do the talking," she said.

That'll be easy, Amy thought. Dan wasn't talking at all.

They were all relieved when they breezed through customs. Halim was a smaller airport for charter flights, so it wasn't too crowded. Within minutes, Nellie had hustled them through the crowd of taxi drivers and picked a blue cab to ride into the city. She worked her cell phone and arranged a hotel room.

"I texted Shep and told him we were safe," she said. "He's going to take a commercial flight and pick up the plane." She shot them a concerned look. "You guys must be exhausted. I've never heard you be quiet for more than thirty seconds. Unless you're asleep."

Dan said nothing, looking out the window at the road lined with palm trees. It was dusk, and lights were beginning to come on. The driver wove through the heavy traffic expertly.

The lights of Jakarta approached. The tall buildings glittered through the heavy air. The skyscrapers seemed impossibly tall, like something out of a science fiction movie. The driver turned off the highway and soon they were on a wide boulevard. The swirling traffic of crowded buses, taxis, and motorcycles whirled them toward a huge circle that surrounded a beautiful fountain. The driver shot off the circle onto a narrower street and gradually, they left the tall buildings behind.

Amy had never been in such a crowded, overwhelming city. She'd thought Cairo was confusing, but this city was a maze, and choked with cars ignoring traffic rules and people dodging between vehicles to cross the traffic-snarled streets. The air was thick and heavy with fumes.

Finally, the driver pulled over in front of a bright orange awning attached to a white building. A doorman hurried out to open the doors and reached for their bags. Nellie counted out the money she'd exchanged at the airport.

They stopped at the desk and Nellie checked them in. "We'd like to arrange a trip to Anak Krakatau tomorrow," she said. "Could you help us with that?"

"Normally, yes," the man said. "But it's off-limits

right now by order of the government. When it goes active, you're not allowed to land on the island."

Amy wanted to burst into tears. Had they come all this way for nothing? Somehow she'd felt that if she could just take a look at the island, they might find something that Robert Henderson had left behind. She had no idea where to start looking for traces of him in Jakarta.

Nellie looked over her shoulder at them. She smiled understandingly, as if she knew how disappointed and tired they were.

"Can we get some American food?" Nellie asked. "Like cheeseburgers?"

Nellie must really be worried about them if she was passing up the opportunity for local food, Amy thought. Then again, Amy herself was worried. Dan was *never* quiet this long.

The clerk smiled. "You can get anything in Jakarta. I can arrange to send food up to your room."

"Cheeseburgers, fries, potato chips . . . whatever you've got," Nellie said.

They took the elevator up to the room and threw down their bags. Amy lifted Saladin from his carrier.

Nellie turned to them. "All right, out with it. What happened? Why aren't you two talking? When I mentioned cheeseburgers, Dan didn't even yelp."

"No reason," Dan said.

"Just tired," Amy mumbled into Saladin's soft fur.

"Sure," Nellie said. "Bad news about Krakatau, but we can think about what to do in the morning. I say we order up a DVD and just hang tonight. I've never been so exhausted." She yawned. "We could maybe go close to the island, but will that tell us anything?" Nellie shook her head. "I'm willing to go, but I'm still not sure what we're looking for."

"I'm not sure, either," Amy said.

"Really?" Dan asked. "I thought you knew everything."

Nellie looked from Dan to Amy, and back to Dan. "'Kay," she said, "I'm making an executive decision. No more talking. Let's eat."

Amy woke up and didn't know where she was. It was pitch-black, and all she heard was a faint hum of air-conditioning. What hotel, what city, what country? A car horn bleated. The room smelled faintly of . . . cheeseburgers. Really bad cheeseburgers.

Jakarta. Java.

The names sounded so foreign as she turned them over in her mind. She doubted that a month ago she could have picked them out on a map. They had flown west from Darwin over the Indian Ocean. Was it possible to be farther away from Boston, Massachusetts? She didn't think so.

She couldn't go back to sleep. Now that her eyes had adjusted, she could just make out the lump that was Dan, over on the sofabed.

She'd hurt Dan. She knew that. All evening she'd

wanted to explain. But explaining would mean confessing. And she couldn't face that night. Talking about it out loud would make the whole thing too real. She'd have to relive it. And if she had to do that, she would break.

She sighed and turned over. Nellie was scrunched over on the side of the wide bed, a pillow half over her head. The edge of the curtain glowed orange from the rising sun. Amy's heart beat faster.

Fire.

"Get the children out!"

She threw the covers back. She clapped her hands over her ears. Inside her head, she was screaming. *Mommy! Don't go!*

She sprang up and walked across the room. She pushed the curtains aside. She saw the sun splashing the tall towers with the start of the day.

She tiptoed over the carpet and sat on the sofabed. "Dan," she whispered.

He kept on sleeping.

"Dan!"

He sat up, confused. "Where are we going? Where are my pants?"

She laughed softly. But the confusion cleared on his face, and the closed look came back.

"I'm sorry I didn't tell you," she said.

"Whatever."

"It's just that—"

"It doesn't matter." Dan threw the covers back.

"So you forgive me?"

"I didn't say that." Dan's mouth was set in a tight line. "Tell me what you remember. Obviously *Irina* knows."

"No, she doesn't! And I don't remember much. It's all weird flashes of stuff. I remember hearing people's voices, and going downstairs, and being afraid because a bunch of strangers were in the house. The voices sounded mean. And Isabel Kabra picked me up . . ." Amy gulped. She couldn't tell Dan about the koalas. He was just absorbing the fact that their parents were murdered by some relative of theirs. What if he knew it was *her fault*?

". . . and I could tell Mom was scared. And I remember later on hearing the front door close and being glad they were gone. And I looked outside and they were standing under my window. Isabel said they had to act that night. Nobody else said anything."

"What do you remember about Mom and Dad?" Dan pressed.

Amy shook her head. "Not much. I remember Mom getting you and me out, and Dad was taking books down from the shelves."

"He was looking for something."

"And then Mom put us on the grass and told me to take care of you, and she ran back inside. And I waited and waited to see them come out. And they didn't." Tears rolled down Amy's cheeks. *Take care of your brother.* It sounded easy. But what was the best way to do it?

Dan looked embarrassed at her tears. "Don't lose it now," he said. "We have work to do."

"You're still talking to me?" Amy asked tearfully.

"I guess so," Dan said. "We're still on a clue hunt. So let's get to work."

Amy pushed away the hurt from Dan's cool tone. Maybe the tension between them would ease. Dan wasn't too good at holding grudges.

She rooted in her backpack. She found packages of peanut butter crackers and tossed one to Dan. "Breakfast."

Dan ripped open the package. "Okay. Last night I tried to figure out how to trace Henderson, but my brain started to hurt. This city is huge. And we have zip for leads."

"I still wish we could see Krakatau," Amy said. "If we could just be where he was, we might figure something out."

"Remember what the desk clerk said when Nellie asked about cheeseburgers?" A little rain of cracker dust spewed out of Dan's mouth when he talked, but Amy wasn't about to mention it. "You can get anything in Jakarta. Maybe if we could just see it, or see what's around it . . . we'd notice something." Dan popped the last cracker in his mouth. "It beats sitting around here."

Amy looked over at the bed, where Nellie was sprawled out, her breathing deep and regular.

"She was so exhausted last night she didn't even listen to her iPod," Amy said. "We can't wake her up.

Let's do a little more research." She reached for Dan's laptop.

Dan flopped back on the bed. "Research? Is that all you can think about?"

"I want to see if there's any more I can find out about that ship. Nellie just flew us over an ocean. We owe her a little sleep."

"Do we?" Dan asked. "I don't know how much we owe her."

"What do you mean?"

"It is funny that we keep finding out stuff about her," Dan said in a low tone. "Remember what you said on the plane?"

"I thought you weren't listening."

"I just wasn't talking to you. I'm *still* not, except when I have to. You said it was like she was trained for this job. You're right."

"I know. And remember that weird message we heard on her cell phone back in Russia? *Call in for a status report . . .* Madame Mysterioso is right." Amy bit her lip. "It's not that I don't trust her. I mean, she's *Nellie.* She's totally cool. It's just that . . . who is she, really?"

"You never know who anybody is," Dan said. "Even the people closest to you. I've learned that for sure."

Amy felt herself blush. She knew Dan wasn't just talking about the Cahills. He was talking about her, too.

Dan glanced over at the sleeping Nellie. "I was thinking . . . if we took a look at her e-mails . . ."

"How can we do that?" Amy asked. "I know she uses your laptop to check in, but she has a password."

Dan looked embarrassed. "Um . . . I memorized it." At Amy's astonished look, he quickly said, "I didn't *mean* to! One morning she was checking e-mail, and I watched her fingers on the keys, and I just . . . remember it."

Dan gave the sleeping Nellie a quick glance. "So all we have to do is log in to her account, and we can plug it in."

"That is so wrong," Amy whispered.

There was a short silence. Amy sighed. "And I wish I'd thought of it first."

She logged on. Dan leaned forward and whispered, "Whoa Nellie." In a moment, they had accessed Nellie's e-mail list. There was a message from her father, *agomez,* saying DONDE ESTAS YOU NOW and a new message from someone called *clashgrrl* at a Boston University e-mail address.

"Look, *clashgrrl* sent Nellie a message yesterday, too," Amy said. "The subject line says 'check in babe.'"

"Probably one of her college friends."

"Sounds like it." Amy clicked on the message. ENTER PASSWORD came up on screen. "That's funny. Are all of her individual e-mails password protected?" Amy clicked on her father's message. *Hola wayward daughter, haven't heard from you since Sydney. Check in with the old man so he can sleep at night. Your admiring*

*and ever-patient father. PS. If you're anywhere near Thailand,
ship me some hot sauce.*

Amy smiled. "Sounds like her dad is a lot like
Nellie."

"Check the rest of the e-mails."

Amy went through them. Nellie had received plenty
of other e-mails from friends and some from her little
sister, but the only ones they couldn't access were from
clashgrrl.

"Why is Nellie getting password-protected messages?" she asked Dan.

They both looked at their sleeping au pair. Just the
top of her head was visible. Without her crackling gaze,
she looked different asleep, like someone they didn't
know.

"Trust no one," Amy whispered. Hadn't they known
that from the very beginning? But *Nellie?* Thinking
that she could be hiding things from them made Amy
feel shaky and off balance, as though the ground was
moving underneath them.

Dan just looked angry. "If she doesn't tell us everything, why should we tell her everything?" He balled
up the cracker wrapper and tossed it in the trash can.
"Let's go find a volcano."

CHAPTER 22

The city of Jakarta had come alive as though at once, in an explosive roar. Outside their hotel, Dan and Amy stood in amazement, watching the trucks, cars, bicycles, and taxis tangle and untangle on the street. Palm trees waved overhead in the breeze, and the sidewalk was packed with people hurrying to work.

"It'll take us hours to get anywhere," Amy said.

Was she always this negative, or did Dan just notice it more when he was mad at her? "Not if we take one of those." Dan pointed down the street. Heading toward them was an orange scooter with three wheels and an open cabin in the back. Dan waved.

"What are you doing?"

"It's a taxi," Dan said. "This thing doesn't have to wait in traffic, either."

The driver pulled over. "You need a *Bajaj*? Easy ride, very cheap, and fast, too. I go everywhere."

"Can you take us to boats?" Dan asked. "Harbor?"

"Harbor, yes, of course. No worries! Hop in!"

They climbed into the back. The driver took off.

170

Amy's head slammed back from the acceleration.

"Sweet!" Dan cried. He couldn't help it.

The scooter dodged between cars and trucks. It made lanes where there were no lanes. It scooted down alleys and rattled through tiny streets. It almost mowed down pedestrians. Dan's head filled with the smell of gasoline and smog, and the noises of the city pressed against him. It was like being in the center of a roaring, rattling machine.

He *loved* Jakarta.

The streets got narrower as their driver zoomed along. Suddenly, they could smell the sea. The driver slowed down, and they passed a market where brightly colored beach umbrellas were stuck in the ground, shading blankets where men in shorts and flip-flops sat selling baskets of fish. They were calling out in high-pitched voices, throwing money around like crazy, and he wished they could stop and check it out.

Ahead they saw masts and colorful sails. The driver pulled up near the harbor. Dan held out a hand filled with crumpled bills, and the driver took some out.

"Do you need a tour?" He swept a hand, taking in the harbor. "I know it all. My cousin owns a fishing boat. Best boat in the harbor, best pilot."

"We want to go to Krakatau," Amy said.

He shook his head. "Active now . . . you can't land on Krakatau."

"Would your cousin . . . take us there? Just to look?" Dan asked.

"Long trip, take all day."

"That's okay."

Dan expected the next words out of the man's mouth to be "Where are your parents?" He knew the guy was *thinking* it. Dan mutely held out a fistful of money.

"Sure," the driver said, grabbing it. "No worries!"

The driver's cousin's name was Darma, and the boat, which seemed good-sized and sturdy at the dock, was suddenly small and flimsy once they'd chugged out into open sea.

Amy and Dan sat in the back watching Darma smiling and pointing out sights. They couldn't hear what he was saying over the motor. He had two men as his crew who spoke no English, but smiled at Amy and Dan if they happened to catch their eyes.

The bow thumped against the sea, and the smell of fish was overpowering. Amy clutched the rail, looking a little green. Dan faced the open water, the wind in his face. The water was a brilliant turquoise, and off to the side he could see a string of islands. Smaller fishing boats tacked across the bay.

After traveling for some time, they saw a point ahead. They were going to round the corner of Java, Dan guessed. He knew Krakatau was to the west.

Darma yelled something at them and laughed. Amy turned to Dan. "What did he say?"

"I think something about Sunday and ships.

Is today Sunday? Did we cross the international date line again? Do I have to repeat fourth grade?"

"He must have said *Sunda*. As in Sunda Strait. After we round the corner of Java, we'll be in it. It's the channel between Java and Sumatra. And it's the way to Rakata. That's the island that Anak Krakatau is on. You see, the island of Krakatau imploded, but another island took its place. It means 'Child of Krakatau,' and—"

"I know you can't help yourself," Dan said. "But please stop."

"Shipping channel!" Darma yelled. This time they heard him perfectly. He smiled and laughed. "When we cross, hang on!"

The water got choppier as they rounded the point. Darma steered the boat closer to the shoreline, and the water smoothed out. The beach looked beautiful, and the hills rose behind them in smoky greens and grays. Across the blue water was Sumatra.

I am on a boat between Java and Sumatra, Dan thought. *How cool is that?*

He was just starting to regret not packing a lunch when the crew set out bowls full of coconut rice. Dan and Amy feasted while they watched the larger cargo ships out in the strait.

The sun was high overhead when Darma signaled to them. "Okay, crossing the strait now." He pointed. "There is Rakata."

They could see it now, the island with the volcanic

peak of Anak Krakatau, the child of Krakatau. Dan felt a chill along his spine.

Darma headed out into the strait, weaving the fishing boat through the busy traffic in the channel with skill. Gigantic cargo ships steamed by, sending their small boat rocking in their wakes. At last they sailed into quieter waters, past islands thick with palm trees and beckoning beaches. They were in the middle of a tropical paradise. It must have looked similar to this when Robert Cahill Henderson first arrived. Except that where the mighty Krakatau once rose from the sea, now a new mountain was rising. It was flat on top, and the white smoke was mixed with gray. Dan heard a rumble of thunder but hardly registered it. He was too much in awe of the sight in front of him. Somehow you could feel the power of it, of how much boiling energy was contained inside.

Even though he'd pretended not to listen, his brain couldn't help but record the facts Amy had read to him back on Shep's plane: 36,000 people died, mostly in the tsunamis that followed the final explosion on August 27; two-thirds of the island was blown away; the final, massive explosion was heard more than 2,000 miles off; shock waves circled the earth seven times; the ash cloud was propelled upward for fifty miles and circled the globe for thirteen days, eventually creating amazing sunsets throughout the following year. All the numbers added up to one bad volcano.

Darma gave the helm to one of his crew and came

back to them. "Not good today," he said. He pointed. "Very active."

Dan saw something sliding down the mountain. Clouds of smoke rose from it as it thundered into the sea. Rocks flew out and splashed so close that Dan could see them. They floated on top of the gentle waves. "Is it erupting?"

"No. But it's not happy," Darma said. "Those are pumice. Not good for the boat."

By the look of the island, Amy and Dan could see that even if they could explore it, they would find nothing. Krakatau had exploded into ash and fire. It had fallen into the sea and vaporized into the air. Seeing the power of the second mountain was enough.

"He must have barely made it out alive," Amy whispered to Dan. "And he lost everything. Everything he worked for."

"No pictures? No video?" Darma asked. "Most tourists do that."

They shook their heads. They didn't need pictures to remember this.

The trip back across the channel was nerve-wracking, but they trusted Darma's handling of the boat and the expert scrambling of the crew. They had hours before they got back, and now there was nothing to do but sit and look at the same shoreline they'd stared at for hours on the way there. The question was, once they got back to Jakarta, what would they do next? Dan almost asked the question out loud, but then he remembered that he was barely talking to his sister. She looked so bummed that he almost forgot how mad he was.

The sun slipped lower in the sky behind them as they finally rounded the point and headed for Jakarta.

Darma came back to talk to them. "Excuse me? We are near the Thousand Islands. Beautiful spot, tourist destination . . ."

"We really have to get back," Amy said.

"Just a little out of your way," Darma said with a wide smile. "I have quick delivery to one island, it won't take long at all!"

Dan shrugged. "I guess it's okay."

They motored through the islands. They could see beautiful houses on some of them, while some were uninhabited.

"He lives on a tiny island, not near the others," Darma explained. "Orders groceries, supplies, things like that. Old man, doesn't say much—my friend took him to Krakatau, just like you! No video for him, either!"

Darma slowed the engine as they chugged toward a lush tropical island. The crew loaded the supplies into a rubber raft. "It will take a moment only," Darma said.

The crew began bringing up supplies from the cabin. Amy sat up.

"Dan," she whispered. "I saw a rosemary plant! Remember Irina's clue?"

Dan turned to Amy. "Okay, this is totally weird, but are you thinking what I'm thinking?"

"That the guy on the island is a Cahill?"

"That the guy on the island is *Robert Cahill Henderson*!"

"That's impossible! He'd be . . . about a hundred and forty years old!"

Dan nodded. "Exactly. Maybe the great Cahill secret is *eternal life.* Or at least a life extender. Think about it, Amy. Wouldn't it make you the most powerful person in the world? Maybe Robert Cahill Henderson didn't go off to die. Maybe he came back here, and for the last fifty years, he's been working on the formula!"

"It's crazy," Amy said slowly.

"It could be true," Dan argued.

They both jumped up. "We're getting off here!" Amy announced. "We'll take the supplies!"

"But there's no hotel here!" Darma protested. "Nothing for tourists!"

"It's okay! We love to camp!" Dan fished in his pocket and came up with more money. He pressed it on Darma. "Pick us up tomorrow, okay?" Dan asked. He slipped out of the boat into the knee-deep water. He picked up one of the boxes and balanced it on his head.

Amy slipped over the rail. She picked up the other box. "Bye!"

Darma hauled the rubber raft aboard. He looked confused. But he shrugged and waved at them. Within moments, his boat had rounded the end of the island and disappeared.

CHAPTER 23

Nellie ran her hands through her hair groggily. She looked at the clock. She couldn't believe that she'd slept for twelve hours.

Naturally, Dan and Amy were gone. And this time, they hadn't even left a note.

She checked her e-mail, and sure enough, there were two messages from *clashgrrl*. She typed in the code and sighed.

KEEP THEM CLOSE. RED ALERT. ARRANGE IMMEDIATE DEPARTURE.

"Now you tell me," Nellie said out loud.

Saladin mewed plaintively. "You, too?" Nellie asked. She scooped him up and petted him absent-mindedly. She couldn't believe she'd lost Amy and Dan again. She'd give them an hour or so before she started to tear her hair out.

Saladin squirmed out of her arms. She was holding him too tight. It was because she was worried. Something didn't feel right.

They were usually good about letting her know when they split. But she'd caught the looks between them when they'd found out she could fly a plane. They were starting to suspect her. Poor little dudes. They couldn't trust anybody.

Another message popped up from *clashgrrl*. The subject line read *don't b lame!*

That meant the message was of the utmost urgency.

Nellie shut the laptop with one bare foot. She wasn't going to check in until she found them. She had a bad feeling about this.

Irina stayed behind as Isabel entered the shop. Isabel had hired a car, but Irina had been able to keep up on a motorcycle. She wore a disguise, but Isabel hadn't taken any of the usual precautions, which meant that she felt safe in Jakarta.

Isabel had a canvas shopping bag that had started out empty and was now bulging with items. Irina had been able to get close enough with the scope in her camera to see what Isabel was buying.

This last item sent a chill through Irina. It was just as she suspected. Isabel had cunning, but not much imagination.

And so here it was. Her last stand would take place here. The power of the 39 Clues could not rest in Lucian hands if Isabel Kabra was the head of the branch.

What would the consequences be if she acted against her leader? She knew very well. She would be cast out. Every Lucian would know that she had betrayed the branch. Isabel and Vikram would make sure of that. They would make up a story, slant things their way. Everything she knew would be gone — money, connections, purpose. The world would become an empty place, and she would become a ghost.

She had no choice. She had to try. *What is the difference between you?* Amy had asked.

This is the difference, Amy. There are some things I will not do. And there are some things I will not allow to happen.

She turned and ran into Ian and Natalie.

Natalie smiled. Irina couldn't see her eyes behind the black sunglasses.

"Good news. My countersurveillance indicates that your mother has not been tailed," Irina said. Not by a flicker of an eyelash would she allow these two hooligans to see they'd unnerved her.

"I have more good news," Natalie said. "Mother received new orders this morning."

"And?"

Stealthily, Irina shot out a needle from each index finger. It would be easier to operate if these two were out of commission for a nice long while.

Natalie moved with such speed that Irina had time for only a flicker of astonishment. She'd always thought of the sulky girl as incapable of zeal. Natalie's hand shot forward, grabbed Irina's finger, and bent it back almost all the way. Irina felt white pain as her finger joint popped. And then the needle sank in.

Amy and Dan dropped the boxes on the beach and trudged up toward the path.

"Why did we let Darma go?" Amy asked. "If we don't find anybody, we'll have to spend the night here."

"That would totally rock," Dan said. "Like Robinson Cruise-o."

"Robinson Crusoe," Amy corrected. They reached the lush tropical forest and struck out on the path.

"I bet Troppo will be glad to see us," Dan said. "We're just one big happy family, right?"

Amy was filled with foreboding. The sun had gone down behind the hill, so the shadows were lengthening. She was suddenly afraid of what they would find.

Dan stepped out into a clearing. "Whoa," he said. "Look at this."

The shell of a large building stood by a stand of palms. Construction equipment still littered the ground, big concrete blocks, thick coils of wire, clay tiles. "It looks like they were going to build a hotel," Dan said. "Look, there are more buildings down there."

"Dan," Amy said. "Look."

She pointed to the sand. Footprints were clearly outlined. Dan put his own foot next to one. The footprint was much larger, the footprint of a man. Amy's doubts about Dan's theory were suddenly crowded out by her fear.

They followed the footprints past the abandoned hotel and through the clearing. Down the path they could see a small crescent beach, the sand colored pink by the setting sun. Tall palms surrounded it. The footprints disappeared, melded into the dimples of the soft sand.

Amy caught a flicker of movement out of the corner of her eye. A hammock was strung between two palm trees. It swayed back and forth gently. She couldn't see the person lying in it, just one bare foot gently pushing the ground to keep it rocking.

They walked closer, hardly breathing. As they reached the hammock, they could see a pair of perfectly pressed lemon-yellow linen shorts. A crisp white shirt. And, his eyes closed, a smile on his face . . . their cousin Alistair Oh.

CHAPTER 24

Alistair opened one eye. If he was surprised to see them, he didn't show it.

"Welcome to paradise," he said.

He swung both legs down so that he was sitting up. "You look disappointed."

"We didn't expect to see you here," Dan muttered.

"I could say the same," Alistair said. "Except it wouldn't be quite true. I'm getting to the point where I'm never surprised when you pop up."

Dan wanted to punch a tree. He was sure he was on the trail of the oldest man in the world. Instead, he'd only found another Cahill cousin.

And he still wasn't sure how he felt about Alistair. Amy had cried when she'd thought Alistair had died in the cave-in back in Korea. Even he had gotten a little damp. Well, okay, he'd cried. A little. But then it turned out Alistair was alive. Which meant he'd totally scammed them. It hadn't been the first time, either. He was an Ekaterina, just as intent on finding the 39 Clues as they were.

Still, he'd helped them in Egypt. It wasn't his fault his submersible — which he'd invented — had sunk. Well, maybe it *was* his fault. They'd almost been fish food under the Nile.

"What are you doing here, Alistair?" Amy asked.

"Same thing you are, I expect," Alistair said. "Trying to figure out what Robert C. Henderson did here. A brilliant man. An Ekat, of course."

"We guessed that," Dan said. "We tracked him in Australia."

"Did you now." Alistair's eyes gleamed. "I'd hate for you to come all the way to Indonesia without satisfying a bit of your curiosity. How about another information exchange? You tell me what you learned in Australia, and I'll tell you what I've learned here. Deal?"

Dan and Amy exchanged a glance. They'd shared information with Alistair before. It usually worked out okay.

"You probably know he was a scientist," Alistair said. "Like so many of our branch, he had a brilliant and inventive mind. He ascended the ranks of the Ekat elite very quickly and attracted the notice of the branch leaders. He was headed for great things. And then he made a great mistake." Alistair paused. "He fell in love with a Lucian."

Dan groaned. "Oh, please. Barf control! Not a love story."

"Yes, a love story. But many love stories are also . . . betrayal stories. She was highborn, a cousin of Queen

Victoria. Which gave the Ekats an idea. There had been a rumor — well, more than a rumor — that about sixty years before a highborn Lucian in the Russian monarchy had assembled most — or even all — of the thirty-nine clues. The Madrigals destroyed his evidence in a raid. But he had retained one copy for safekeeping. It was passed to Lucian headquarters in London sometime in the 1880s. We suspect that the Madrigals killed Tsar Nicholas II and his family in 1918, searching for that list. But that's another story. Only the Ekats knew that the list had been passed to London."

Amy didn't look at Dan. Dan didn't look at Amy. They had found the evidence of the assembled Clues back in Russia, but they weren't about to tell Alistair that.

"However — and this is so typically Lucian — even if they had been able to steal and trick enough to get so many, they didn't have the skill to figure out *amounts*. That is a job for the Ekats. So they gave Robert Henderson a choice. His fiancée's father was the branch leader of the Lucians. If Robert didn't spy on him and try to ascertain whether the Lucians had the thirty-nine clues, he would be kicked out of the Ekats forever."

Amy gasped. "That's terrible!"

Alistair turned his dark eyes on her. "After all this time, all this effort, you *still* don't understand how important this is, do you?"

"I do. It's just that —"

He shook his head. "No. If you truly understood what was at stake, you would know that it's sometimes necessary to be ruthless. At any rate, Robert Henderson was torn. Apparently, he was deeply in love. But he was *also* something else—a scientist. The temptation to find the clues and assemble them—he couldn't resist that challenge. So he successfully stole the only copy of the clues the Lucians had. Naturally, they knew perfectly well it was he who had done it, so . . . the marriage was off. The Ekats got him on a ship to the South Seas and made up a story about him following Darwin. But he really went to Indonesia. Then, of course, he made his fatal mistake. He built his lab on a known volcano. There were reasons for it—it was uninhabited, and he was able to harness its geothermal energy to power his lab. He was an Ekat, after all. He was taking a chance, and he knew it. Of course, he lost the gamble."

"What happened?" Amy asked. "I mean, we know that Krakatau erupted, but where was he?"

"Ah, the Krakatau eruption. Who knows what triggered it? Some Ekats believed the Madrigals blew up Henderson's lab, which started a deadly geothermal chain of explosions. But Henderson? He was lucky. He was on his way to collect a shipment he had ordered for the lab. He knew that the volcano was active. There had been considerable activity on the island, earthquakes, steam . . . he knew very well the danger he faced. But he was close. So agonizingly close that he left the island at the last possible second — the night before the main eruption. He barely made it out alive, and his laboratory blew up in one of the first eruptions. That's when he got burned. That next morning he was across the strait in the coastal town of Anjer when the tsunami came. He ran up into the hills to escape it. The population tried to outrun this gigantic, overpowering wave a hundred feet tall . . . can you imagine the terror? Hundreds were sucked back into the sea or pummeled against the rocks. He saw horror and suffering and he made it out alive. We know he went to Jakarta. We know weeks later he booked passage to Sydney. We lost track of him after that. We think his mind was broken. He just . . . disappeared." Alistair turned to them. "So. Did you find him?"

"We found out that he was in jail," Amy said. "They called him Bob Troppo. We traced him to a place called Coober Pedy, where he became an opal miner called Fossie. He died in the 1950s. But he never said another word. Or left a hint. Just a bunch of gibberish on the walls of a mine."

"But he did leave a hint," Alistair said. "I know because I have it."

"Where did you get it?"

"Ah," Alistair said. His gaze slid away from them. "Perhaps that revelation should be left for another time."

"Can we see it?"

Alistair took an old paper out of his shirt pocket. "If

you figure it out, we share the clue. Agreed?" After they nodded, he handed it to Dan and Amy.

Far from home I set up my endeavour
Risked all — love, even life, to sever
If need be. Yet with all I had
The Clues given, brain nearly mad
With knowledge gained and lost
   and gained again
With chance and right to rule all men
I failed. By merely one, cruel fate
Left for me to calculate.

The very waves sang the song I knew
Though I knew it not. Merely rue.
One morn despair to me befell
In a fit I could not dispel
To have come so far and risked it all
To try, to fail, to fall.

I threw myself upon the strand
This exile I could scarce withstand
And yet then at the blackest hour
There, as in Newton's bower
The answer thundered down.
The price? A sodden crown.
Reward? Ah, 'tis merely this:
End and answer, elixir, bliss.

"Well, *that* clears everything up," Dan said.

"I think I get part of it," Amy said. "He left every-thing behind, risked his life, in order to put together the thirty-nine clues. And he almost got the answer—he was missing one only clue. *By merely one, cruel fate/Left for me to calculate.*"

"He was wrong about that," Alistair said. "We know he didn't actually have thirty-eight clues. But he was close. Very close."

"But what does it mean that the waves sang a song and he knew it but he didn't know it?"

"It means he'd already gone troppo," Dan said. He groaned. "I'm flashing back to Mrs. Malarkey's English class, and it's not pretty. What's rue?"

"It means sadness," Alistair said. "He tried so hard and for so long, and he came so close, but he lost. But here's the part I can't figure out. He's in despair, so he comes and throws himself on the *strand*—a fancy word for beach. Then all of a sudden he's talking about Newton. Was there something that Newton discovered that he needed? I know he figured out gravity, but what does it have to do with the thirty-nine clues?"

"*The price? A sodden crown,*" Amy repeated. "What does that mean? That he was almost king of the world or something?"

"Crown can mean 'head,' too," Alistair said. "As in 'Jack fell down and broke his crown' but it still doesn't make sense to me. I believe the reference is to the story of Newton—that he thought of gravity when he was lying under a tree and an apple fell on his head. So he could be saying that he had a sudden revelation. But why doesn't he say what it is?" Alistair sighed. "Maybe he was already losing his mind."

"Ya think?" Dan asked.

A strong breeze rattled the paper. It had grown suddenly dark. The palm trees were bending with the gusts.

"It's going to storm," Alistair said. "We'd better get inside. Don't worry, these tropical storms blow themselves out quickly. I can call for a launch and get you home in time for dinner."

CHAPTER 25

Hours later, Dan stared out at the pounding rain. The palm trees were bending like dancers. From here he could just make out the white line of the surf. The sun had set long ago. They were trapped for the night.

"Not exactly blowing over," he said. "More like blowing."

"Who knew?" Alistair said sheepishly. "I haven't been watching the weather. As soon as I get a clear signal, you can call Nellie. There's plenty of room here for you to spend the night."

Alistair was staying in the only finished house on the island, on the edge of the construction site. It had been planned as a resort, but the Ekaterinas had bought it as a site for a possible stronghold. They were still deciding whether to finish it, but, in the meantime, Alistair came now and then.

The house had one large room downstairs that was open on all sides and had a double-height ceiling. Alistair had closed sturdy wooden shutters when they had come up from the beach. Upstairs was a complete living area, with two bedrooms, a sitting room, and a small kitchen.

The rain was still pattering lightly while they finished a meal of vegetables and rice. Alistair tried Nellie on his phone and she answered. He put her on speaker.

"Who is this?" she barked.

"It's Alistair Oh, Ms. Gomez. I'm calling to tell you that Dan and Amy are here with me and—"

"Are they safe?"

"We're safe, Nellie!" Amy called.

"I'll come and get them."

"No need. The weather—"

"I don't care about the weather! Where are you?"

"Nellie, we're on an island. We'll be back in the morning," Amy said. She could hear real concern in Nellie's voice. "We're sorry we didn't leave a note."

"We can talk about the fact that you *totally freaked me out for an entire day* another time. Right now I'm coming to get you."

"Ms. Gomez—Nellie—I'm afraid you will have to wait until morning," Alistair said reluctantly. "I swear I will deliver the children to you myself."

"Don't bother. I'll be there tomorrow morning."

After Alistair gave her directions and assurances that he'd fed them dinner and Dan had chimed in about the sad lack of dessert, Nellie said a reluctant good night and she'd see them tomorrow. *Early.*

"Now, I think it's been a long day and we should all retire," Alistair said in his formal way. "You'll be safe here tonight."

A few minutes later, Amy did feel safe as she snuggled under the cotton quilt. Alistair had loaned them each one of his soft white cotton T-shirts to wear to bed because their clothes still smelled like fish and saltwater. The wind and rain had stopped, and a fresh breeze wafted through the window. Amy fell asleep listening to the faint rustling of the palms. Far away, a motor softly purred out on the dark sea. She was so tired that she hoped she wouldn't dream.

At first she thought she was still hearing the whisper of the leaves outside. The noise was so soft. She turned over and felt herself slipping back into sleep. She could still smell the smoky trace of their dinner. . . .

She sat up. She could smell it now. She could see the wisps of smoke curling in the moonlight.

Panic shot through her. But she couldn't seem to move. She was seeing another night, another time.

Fire. Amy holds her mother's hand. She cries as they run down the stairs to the first floor. "Get the children out!" her father shouts. He's in the den, pulling books down off the shelves. Looking for something . . . "Daddy!" she screams. She holds out her arms and he stops for a second. "Angel," he says, "go with Mommy."

"No!" She sobs as her mother pulls her away. "No! Daddy!"

"Arthur!" her mother shouts. But she continues on with Amy and Dan.

Cool night air, damp grass against her bare legs. Her mother leans over her. She takes Amy's face in her hands. "Look at me," her mother says, the way she always does when she wants Amy to listen hard. "Take care of your brother. I love you." Amy screams, begs her to come back even as her mother races back into the burning house. . . .

She was so intensely part of the memory that it wasn't until she started to cough that she realized fully this wasn't a dream. The house was on fire!

Alistair appeared in the doorway. She saw the shadows of flames flickering on his face, and it sent a jolt through her body.

Alistair was there that night, too.

He had damp towels in his hands, just like her mother had on that night so long ago. He closed the bedroom door and put the wet towel against the crack. Then he bent over double, coughing.

He was standing next to the fireplace, his face in shadow. Pants ironed to a knife-crease. Gray suit, bright yellow tie. He coughed politely. "Let's calm down. We are only here to take what is ours."

Dan sat up in bed, coughing. The sound of his distress helped Amy to move.

She threw off the sheet.

Alistair rushed toward Dan. He pressed the wet towel against Dan's face. He put an arm around him and started to lead him to the window. "Hurry!" he called over his shoulder to Amy.

When she got to the window, she saw smoke rolling out from below. She looked behind and saw the eerie sight of smoke blasting through the cracks surrounding the closed door. There would be no escape that way.

"The ledge," Alistair said.

Outside the window was a ledge wide enough to stand on. She heard the sound of shattering glass as the window blew out in the room next door. Alistair stepped out on the ledge and held out a hand to Dan. "Come on. The wind is blowing the smoke the other way. You can breathe out here."

Dan stepped out onto the ledge. He gulped in the fresh air. Amy stepped out next. The wall behind her back was hot.

She looked down. Far below was the construction debris. Twisted coils of wire, concrete, nails, tangles of rusty rebar. There was no clear place to land. Even if they could survive the jump, they could be impaled on the sharp objects. Dan's breathing was heavy and constricted. Alistair kept his arm around him. The flames roared. No help was coming. No sirens.

"I'll jump," Alistair said. "Maybe I can find a ladder or something. I'll find a way to get you down."

"You can't jump!" Amy cried. "You'll be killed!"

He smiled as he touched her cheek briefly. "It's our only chance."

Alistair braced himself against the wall. He looked

IN TOO DEEP

down, searching for a clear spot to land. There was none.

"Wait!" Amy hung on to his sleeve. "Look!"

"Irina," Dan said.

The smoke rolled and cleared, and they saw her running below, fast and strong, her legs pumping. She had a bamboo pole in her hand. As they watched in astonishment, she dug the pole into the ground and made a spectacular vault up to the roof.

They heard the soft thump as she landed. Amy leaned out. She could just make out Irina above. Irina slid the pole down and steadied it against the lip of the roof.

"What is the word?" she called to them. "Shimmy? Shimmy down the pole! One at a time, it's not very strong."

"Can we trust her?" Alistair asked Dan and Amy.

It was Amy who spoke. She kept her eyes on Irina's intent face.

"Yes," she said.

Dan went first. He wrapped his legs around the pole and half slid, half shimmied down. As soon as he hit the ground, Amy took a deep breath of relief.

"Go, Amy," Alistair said.

Amy turned and put her hands on the pole. She looked up at Irina, who was lying flat on the roof, steadying the pole with both hands. Irina winced, and Amy saw a red and swollen finger.

"Wait. Before you go," Irina said. "Take this."

She held out one hand. Amy reached up. Grace's necklace dropped into her palm.

"Isabel did it again," Irina said. "The first time, I walked away. Not this time. This time, I will not let her succeed. Now . . . everything is up to you and Dan. *Go!*"

The force of Irina's words propelled Amy into action. She grabbed the bamboo pole. It felt hot against her hands, but she slid down.

She looked up at Alistair. He saluted Irina, then grabbed the pole and winced. Amy saw smoke curling up. The pole was starting to burn. Alistair quickly shimmied down, jumping off the last few feet.

The pole burst into flame. Slowly, it toppled down. Amy, Dan, and Alistair leaped out of the way as it crashed inches away from them.

"We need to find another pole!" Alistair shouted.

They wrenched their eyes from the burning building. They scanned the area frantically, moving through the debris. Dan headed to search in the grove. Somewhere, they had to find something to save her.

From high above, Irina watched them. The roof was so hot now it was agony to stand on it. The smoke rolled across her and cleared. She felt so far away from them. How hopeful they were. They didn't know yet that it was too late.

Half the roof collapsed in a shower of sparks. Fire

was roaring, eating up the wood beams. She inched away.

She had only seconds. That was all right. She'd saved him. She'd saved her beloved boy.

No, not Nikolai. Dan. Dan and Amy.

She struggled to keep her mind clear. The smoke was burning her eyes, her throat. It was a great effort to keep standing. She would keep standing.

She would die a better person than she'd lived. That wasn't too bad, for an ex-KGB spy, not to mention a Cahill.

Look, they are still searching for a pole, hoping to save me. How nice to see that. Poor Alistair, he never liked me, but there was that one night in Seoul when he let down his guard and I let down mine, and we shared a bowl of bibim-bap. One bowl, two spoons. Every time I clinked against his spoon by accident he would accuse me of flirting with him. Finally, he got me to laugh. . . .

Sudden panic seized her. Was she really ready to let go of life? There was a way to live that was not her way—she'd had glimpses of it. With Nikolai and . . . a few others. What agony it was to let it go! It was letting go of possibility. Of a dream.

I hope they know it was worth it to me, she thought, staring at the Cahill children. *Remember what I said, children. Fear her. In your hands it all lies now.*

The roof gave a great crack and roar—and collapsed. Irina cried out as she felt herself fall, and she looked up. She wanted her last sight to be the stars.

CHAPTER 26

Amy and Dan sat on the beach the next morning, looking out at the calm tropical waters. They had spent the longest night of their lives, unable to sleep, just sitting, waiting for dawn. Now they stared with bloodshot eyes out at the horizon. Their white T-shirts were gray from smoke and soot, and their throats still felt dry and scratchy despite the water they'd drunk.

They knew Nellie would be here soon on a launch. It was important they leave before the authorities arrived. Alistair had ordered them to stay on the beach. He didn't want them to see what remained at the house. They didn't want to think about it.

He had wandered off, and they knew he wanted to be alone. Irina had been his enemy, but he'd known her a long time. Maybe he wanted to mourn her.

Irina had been their enemy, too. Last night, she had saved their lives.

Amy touched the jade dragon on her necklace. Why? How could someone she'd thought of as pure evil have the goodness inside to sacrifice her life for them?

Last night someone had stolen the poem. Alistair knew that much. He had awakened, smelled smoke, and immediately checked for the paper. They all knew it had to be Isabel. Alistair had heard the sound of a motor out on the water, but he hadn't been able to see anything.

This morning they'd found the vessel that no doubt Irina had used, a small fishing boat she'd probably paid someone to borrow back at the harbor.

They had the facts, or most of them. What they couldn't sift through was their feelings.

The only thing Amy knew for sure was that it was time to tell Dan. She had to tell him now, before Nellie showed up. She couldn't go through another day like yesterday. She could face anything, but she couldn't face it without Dan.

She'd been so wrong, and he'd been so right. He'd been so scared last night, but he'd never lost his nerve. He'd been like that all along. Times when she was frozen with fear, he'd kept on moving. In so many ways, he was braver than she was.

He could face anything.

"There's a reason I didn't tell you about Mom and Dad being murdered," she said haltingly. "And it wasn't because I didn't trust you. It was because I remembered something I did. I didn't want you to know. I-I didn't want you to blame me."

He shot her a questioning look.

"That night . . . the night of the fire . . . I was still awake when the strangers came. I heard them downstairs.

I listened at the door. They were asking Mom and Dad where they'd been. They asked over and over." Amy paused, and then the words rushed out. "I was scared. S-so I ran inside the room. A woman picked me up. Isabel. She talked about the teddy bears on my night-gown and I corrected her. I said they were koalas. So that's how they all knew."

Dan shook his head. "Knew what?"

"That Mom and Dad had gone to Australia in search of Robert Cahill Henderson. And they must have fig-ured that they'd brought something back. Because later, when they were outside, Isabel said, *They traced him to Australia, didn't they? This has to be taken care of tonight.*"

"Do you think that they did bring something back? And that's what Dad was looking for?"

"What do you do when your house is on fire?" Amy asked.

"You run for the most valuable thing. So Mom ran for us, and Dad ran for whatever it was."

"Maybe somebody set the fire so they could watch what happened. Maybe things went wrong. But the fire wouldn't have happened if I hadn't told them that Mom and Dad were in Australia! If I hadn't been such a . . . know-it-all!" Amy buried her face in her hands. Her shoulders shook with sobs. She felt as though she could cry forever. She could cry out her grief and her shame but it would keep welling back up, and it would never stop.

Dan squirmed. "Amy. Wigging. Totally."

She lifted her head, swiping a hand across her eyes. "What?"

"Let me get this straight. Because you had koalas on your pajamas, our parents died?"

"Well . . ."

"That's just dumb. Our parents died because our house caught fire. You didn't light the match. One of our dear, devoted relatives did. You dweeb. You think that because you said the magic word, you changed everything? We're talking *Cahills* here. They would have done it no matter what."

The scorn in Dan's voice took away Amy's fear. If Dan had been soothing, if he'd tried to reassure her, she would have lost it again. Soot still streaked his pale face. He looked tired, worn out, sad. And honest.

"You are one awesomely weird sister-dude," Dan said.

She wanted to hug him, but she knew it would totally freak him out. She hugged her knees instead. She felt a little of her shame begin to lift. Dan saw things clear. If he didn't think she was to blame . . . maybe she wasn't. She had said the words out loud, she had dredged up every memory, and she hadn't shattered.

Instead, Amy realized, the opposite had happened. She was *stronger*.

"Irina said something else in the tunnel," she said. "She asked me why Mom ran back into the house. Was it just for Daddy? What could be more important than their children?"

"The fate of the world?" Dan joked.

But his grin faded as he met Amy's serious green eyes.

"The fate of the world," she repeated.

They didn't say anything for a minute. It seemed impossible to think about right now, with the smudge of pink on the horizon and the lightening blue of the sea. Impossible to think of the great, wide world around them . . . depending on *them*.

"I think I know what they were looking for," Dan said. "The poem."

"Alistair stole it," Amy said. "It all makes sense now. Last night I remembered him standing by the fireplace. While everyone was looking at me, he was looking at the books."

"Where they'd hidden the poem."

"I bet Mom and Dad thought the poem could lead to *lots* of clues," Amy said. "And they sacrificed themselves to save it."

"If Alistair was there that night, he could have been in on the plan to start the fire," Dan said.

"Not Alistair!"

"Why not?" Dan asked. "Remember what he said to you yesterday? That when so much is at stake, it's okay to be ruthless? We can't say it wasn't him."

"If only we could figure out the poem," Amy said. "There's got to be a clue hidden in it. I wish the answer would thunder down on *my* head. Like last night, during the storm . . ."

Dan frowned and looked out at the sea. Suddenly, he slapped the sand and began to laugh.

"Have *you* gone troppo?" Amy asked.

Dan jumped up and down in front of Amy. "It's just like Mrs. Malarkey said." Dan put on a falsetto voice. "Class, don't be scared by the fancy language. Find the meaning."

"So?" Amy waved her hand in the air. "Mrs. Malarkey? I still don't get it."

"The poem! The dude is feeling bummed out, and he's sitting on the beach, and it starts to rain, okay? And rain comes down on his head."

"I got that much."

"But it also makes him think. *The very waves sang the song I knew.* What does he keep talking about?" At Amy's blank look, Dan pointed. "Water!"

"Water is the clue?" Amy asked. "Could it be that easy?"

"That's why the dude was so happy and so mad at himself at the same time," Dan said. "It *is* that easy."

Amy frowned. "We promised to tell Alistair."

"Even though we know he was at the house that night and could have murdered our parents?" Dan asked. "I'd call that a deal breaker."

"Last night he was willing to jump off that ledge to save us," Amy said.

"Or himself," Dan said. "I say we wait until we know for sure what happened that night."

"Shhh," Amy said, because she saw Alistair heading

toward them. His silk pajamas were stained with soot and dirt, and tufts of hair stood out from his head.

He faced the rising sun. "It's a good day," he said. "We're alive."

He looked sad and funny, Amy thought, in his pink pajamas and his cotton candy hair. How could he be a murderer? But Dan was right. They couldn't just hand him a Clue. Not yet.

They heard the faint sound of a motor. Out beyond the reef, a boat was approaching. They could see an arm waving frantically. Nellie.

Alistair waved back. He walked to the edge of the sea.

They watched as Alistair stood, the cuffs of his sooty pajama bottoms getting wet, the breeze blowing his gray hair. The man they were fond of, whom they couldn't trust, was waving at the au pair they were learning to love . . . and whom they couldn't trust.

"Things are getting complicated," Dan said.

"I wish I could remember who else was there!" Amy burst out. "Maybe more flashes will come back to me. I can't stand not knowing."

Dan's face hardened. "We have to find out who did it for sure. Isabel set the fire, but we need to know who else was there."

"And then what?" Amy asked. "What do we do? Call the cops?" She gave a weird strangled laugh.

"I don't know yet," Dan said. "But they have to pay."

"Revenge sounds so . . . Cahill," Amy said.

"Not revenge," Dan said. "Justice."

They looked at each other. Amy felt the presence of her parents, closer than they'd ever been, and the ghost of Irina saying, *It's all up to you now.*

She and Dan were together again. There were no secrets between them. There never would be again. She could see that he knew it. Behind his eyes, trust was back.

And on this sad morning, sitting on a tropical beach with ruins smoking behind them, with Irina's last cry still ringing in their ears, they made a promise to each other without speaking. A vow. They wouldn't rest until they had exposed who had murdered their parents.

They had started on the hunt for the 39 Clues for Grace's sake. Now they would win it for Arthur and Hope.

"Justice," Amy agreed.